Green Ivy Publishing
1 Lincoln Centre
18W140 Butterfield Road
Suite 1500
Oakbrook Terrace IL 60181-4843
www.greenivybooks.com

ISBN: 978-1-944680-64-0

To the love of my life, who believed in me even when I didn't.

BURNING FIELDS

by

Nathan Brown

Chapter One: An Unexpected Visitor

Philadelphia, Pennsylvania House of Blake Sampson

Dusk June 9, 2015

Blake Sampson slowly got out of his chair, and looked out the window of his one story home. Nightfall was coming shortly. He sighed, went to his cupboard, and pulled out a bottle of whiskey. He got a glass from the cabinet and poured himself a few fingers of the liquid and sipped on it.

Two years ago today, he thought, *was the day...* He stopped thinking about it and took another long sip from the whiskey. He sat back down and lost himself in thought and drink.

A few hours slipped by and he woke with a start; someone was knocking on the door. Blake got up and walked over to the door. He looked through the peeping hole and saw a man dressed in all black and with the exception of an Indianapolis Colts hat.

Blake opened the door and found a Beretta staring him in the face. Blake lifted his arms slowly saying, "I'm unarmed, sir. Please just take what you want."

The man removed his hat and stepped into the light. "You know why I'm here Sampson." the man said menacingly.

Blake gasped, "Jacob! No, you're dead! You're dead Jacob! I saw you die in the explosion! Jacob, I'm sorry! I was ordered to do it! You knew the risks!" He was frantically trying to buy time, to convince this man that it wasn't his fault. "Jacob, you're supposed to be dead!" he said terrified.

Jacob Fields stood at the doorway and walked inside a little further. He closed the door, not once lowering his gun. He looked his old friend dead in the eyes, "Sorry to disappoint," and squeezed the trigger.

Chapter Two: The Agent

Philadelphia, Pennsylvania Rural Residential Area

Morning June 10

Police gathered outside the house. Several police officers walked about trying to keep civilians back and keep order around the building. Another vehicle, a jet black SUV, pulled up to the crime scene and three men and one woman got out.

The officer in charge approached them, "I'm Lieutenant Branson, what are you doing here?" The female redhead in black took out her badge; the acronym CIA was perfectly visible.

Branson looked the woman over, she seemed like a no nonsense type of person. She looked at him and firmly stated, "Lieutenant, I'm Agent Kathryn Madison of the CIA and we will be taking over this investigation. Tell me everything you've gathered."

Branson knew better than to argue with her so he just nodded and led the CIA team into the house where they walked into a trashed room. He led the agents to a corner of the house and then turned to face the CIA team. "From what we've gathered," he started, "we've determined that this was a break in and this poor sod got in the way." He walked over to the body of the man lying in the middle of the floor and crouched next to it. He looked up to Madison, "If I may ask, what in the hell brings the CIA here for this homicide?"

Madison gave him a curt reply, "Classified. Did anyone witness the crime?" Branson just gave a "hmph" and continued examining the body.

"Not a one. Whoever shot this man must have done it at an extreme close range." He lifted the dead man's head and pointed to the middle of his forehead. "Shot residue and scorch marks. I'd say he was shot as soon as the other person walked in. There's a destroyed laptop in the other room, no idea what was on it."

Madison looked at the body and said, "Thank you Lieutenant that will be all." She watched the unhappy and aggravated man walk out the door, then turned to her team, "Harrison what do you think our killer was after?"

Lloyd Harrison, a good agent though his hair was a little longer than standard regulation, and always trying to impress. He stood next to her, "Hell if I know, ma'am. Place is a scattered mess, hard to tell if anything is actually even missing." The agent ran his hands through his hair annoyed. "Sampson always was one for keeping secrets, so I'd say someone wanted to desperately find something." Harrison moved around the room trying to find a clue as to what happened. "You two, make sure that no one enters the house uninvited." The two other agents, following orders, walked outside to man the doorway.

Madison moved around the house looking for something, anything that could help identify why someone would break into a retired agent's home. She went over to what seemed to be the library of the house. There was the laptop that the officer mentioned, sitting on top of a desk, shot to pieces. "Harrison, I think I got the laptop." She showed him the ruined computer, "Think our computer genius can find out what may have been on it?"

Harrison looked over the laptop, "Can try to, it'll take a while in that condition though." He suddenly grew worried, "Do you think he had many important documents left on there?"

Madison looked at Harrison, "I hope not, I'm counting on the fact that he erased everything after he received orders." She went over to the victim's body and examined Blake one more time. "We'll need to take his body to the lab and extract the bullet. That'll give us something anyway." She stepped away from Blake's body.

Harrison puzzled, "Could this be connected to the breach in security we had a year ago?"

"It's possible, but doubtful," Madison replied "it wouldn't make sense because we locked it down after only a few short seconds of the breach. Even an experienced hacker would need at least two minutes to obtain anything of worth."

She looked around the room one more time. *This had been a clean hit, in and out fairly quickly. A professional hit maybe? But who would want Blake dead, and what did he have that the killer wanted?* She concluded to herself that no questions would be answered until they were back at headquarters.

Chapter Three: The Office

Langley, Virginia Central Intelligence Agency Headquarters

Evening June 13

Harrison briskly walked over to Madison's desk and planted the case file on her desk, "Nothing, nada, zilch! Not a single damn lead." He pulled up a swivel chair and sat next to her desk.

Madison picked up the file and shuffled through it, "You're kidding me? Not a single thing off of the forensics sweep of the bullet?"

"Not a single clue, untraceable. Our only hope is that something turns up on the laptop, though that's a slim chance." He gave a long sigh and then put his head on her desk.

Madison grabbed a ruler off her desk and slapped him on the head with it. "Ow!" Harrison jerked up and rubbed his head, "What was that for?"

"For snoozing, we have no idea what this person may have obtained off of that laptop." She started to get angry, "This represents a major security breach and I, for one, will not have it on my record." Madison knew what her job entailed and she wasn't about to screw up. "I'm heading down to the genius tank and see if they found anything yet."

—~—

Jacob Fields, now in the guise of an agent of the CIA, wearing a black suit and tie, walked with dignity down the hallway of the organization he used to work for. He walked past an attractive redhead and smiled and winked as she walked by. With her out of sight, he moved at a brisk pace and looked around for a concealed office. He found one at the end of the hallway. It was easy enough to gain access to their headquarters; Blake had neither deleted the access codes to get in nor deleted some other important codes that Fields required.

He sat at a computer and began to type in the required codes to get into the system. He didn't have much time before they knew that "Sampson" was back in H.Q. *In, now just download names and files...*

—ᨓ—

Madison passed a man on her way to see about the progress on the laptop. He was dressed up in a black suit and he winked at her, she suddenly became annoyed, *typical man,* she thought. She turned around to get another glimpse of the man, but he was no longer there. She waved the thought aside, for there were more important matters to attend to. She entered an elevator and it quickly sank into the basement of Headquarters.

The technician tank came into view as the elevator doors opened. The door to the technician tank needed special access to proceed, so she swiped her I.D. and entered the room. Madison quickly asked, "Baker, how's that laptop coming?"

Linda Baker, the leading computer technician was short, had green eyes, and brown hair. She made up for her height with her computer knowledge, at least that's how she put it.

"Not much to give you Kathryn," Linda always used first names instead of last names, "The system has been practically fried." She led Madison over to the laptop, "This laptop was essentially told to self-destruct and then it was shot for good measure." Linda laughed to herself, "Looks like this ghost of yours didn't want anything getting back to him, however, lucky for you, I'm a genius."

"Give me something Baker," Madison said eagerly.

"I was able to pull some data, though not much, from the laptop. The only thing I could retrieve was the last copied document." Linda typed on her computer and a document popped up. "You're not going to like it Kate."

Kate walked over to the screen, and gave it a good long stare. She didn't realize her mouth gaped open, "These are access codes to Headquarters, here!" She read through more lines of information, "these are also computer codes to get into our system!" *The man!* With that thought she raced off from the technician room, grabbed her phone, and dialed.

Linda called to her, "I guess I'll take that as a thank you!"

Harrison answered his phone, "Yeah boss?"

"Code Red! We have a security breach, Level Alpha!" She said panicking.

"Oh shit!" He took a few short breaths and Madison heard typing, "Madison, I ran security checks; it says that Blake Sampson entered the building ten minutes ago!"

—∾—

Jacob was tapping his foot and speaking out loud to himself, "come on, come on, come on!" The computer seemed to be taking forever.

The computer screen finally read:

FILES COPIED

DOWNLOAD COMPLETE

"About time," Jacob pulled the flash drive out of the computer and then alarms began to sound. *Damn,* he quickly left the room, closed the door, and began walking at a fast pace to the exit.

People were running all over the place, everyone was confused and in a panic. Over his shoulder Jacob heard the sound of a Glock 42 click. "Freeze," a female voice cried out.

Jacob removed a small switch from his coat pocket and hid it in his fist. He slowly turned to face his adversary. It was the redhead who he passed in the hall only a few minutes ago. *That's what I get for winking at a pretty girl, karma,* Jacob thought with a smirk.

Madison was in no mood for games, "Put your hands up!" She said as she steadily aimed her gun at the man before her.

"Are you so sure you want me to do that?" He smiled and raised his hands. Jacob slowly revealed that he had a small remote in his hand. He pressed it.

Madison yelled, "Everybody down!" A loud, BANG, went off and all Madison saw was a blinding light. She pulled the trigger and felt the gun vibrate in her hands. She felt defenseless, all she heard was ringing, and all she could see was white light. She fell over herself and struggled to get up, the effect of the flash bomb slowly wearing off as she tried running after the intruder.

—ꟺ—

Jacob was fast, he knew that, but this woman was right on his tail. He turned a corner and encountered three armed personnel who had responded to the code red.

Jacob, with lightning quick reflexes, grabbed the gun of the closest threat and twisted the gun around his finger. Jacob heard the bone snap as the man yelped. Jacob ripped the gun from him and hit the man's temple rendering him unconscious. He then rolled underneath an attacker's arm and kicked out. Jacob's foot landed on the side of the man's knee and split the joint. He slammed his fist between the spine and the neck putting him out of the fight.

The final man landed a punch on Jacob's torso. Jacob staggered back and the man tried a punch to his face. He leaned back and the man had a clear miss. Jacob punched his enemy's kidney and landed another fist straight in the other man's throat. Seven seconds had ticked by and Jacob was back on the run.

—~—

Madison ran after the intruder and witnessed him take out three agents, including Harrison. She ran over to him with a concerned look. She knelt by him and got him to his feet. He was gasping for air, "He... hit me in the throat." His speech was raspy. Madison, all the more angry now, ran off after the man.

She finally made it outside and looked around and saw him high tailing it out of the area. She took off after him with a great amount of speed.

The man entered an alleyway with Madison in close pursuit. She took out her weapon and shot off a few rounds towards him. She saw a single bullet impact his right shoulder blade. The man didn't even seem to notice and continued at the same speed. He rounded a corner as Madison chased after him and turned the corner that he had only seconds before.

The next thing she saw was a lead pipe hitting her across the stomach and a punch to her face. She fell to the ground, felt a stinging pain beneath her skull, and went unconscious.

—~—

"Madison! Madison! Damnit, KATE!" Agent Madison opened her eyes and saw Harrison right in her face.

"Good Lord, I heard you the first time," Madison said annoyed. She lifted her body up and groaned. Her entire body ached. She felt across her stomach and figured she had one, maybe two cracked ribs. Next, her hands went to her face, she had a bruised cheek bone. The worst of all her injuries was on the base of her skull. A knot had formed where she fell to the ground and bumped her head, giving her a massive headache.

Harrison looked her over, instantly concerned, "Damn he beat you pretty bad. We need to get you to a hospital."

"No, I don't need a hospital, just get me back to H.Q. Help me up." Madison said in a painful voice. She held out her arms and Harrison assisted her in standing up. Madison yelled in pain. He put her arm around his shoulders, he put his around her waist, and she limped back to CIA Headquarters.

Harrison asked, "Who the hell was that?"

Madison looked over at him, "I don't know," She said in a vengeful voice, "but he just picked the wrong lady to hit."

Chapter Four: The Stitching

Washington D.C. Jacob Field's Apartment

Midnight June 14

Jacob Fields sat in his bathroom with a trauma kit. He looked into the mirror to see his back. He needed to get the bullet out. That redhead was a good shot, perhaps he could use her in the days to come, but first things first.

Fields took a large set of tweezers and plunged into the wound, trying to extract the bullet. He looked over his shoulder so he could get a better view. Attempt after attempt he tried to grab the bullet, but it wasn't working.

"Shit, time to use the knife." As he spoke to himself he brought out the sharp blade. He gritted his teeth as he slowly dug the projectile out, and flung it across the bathroom. Fields gasped as he finally pried the bullet free.

Jacob took the stitching equipment out and began to work. He looked over his shoulder when it was all over, *Not too bad if I do say so myself.*

He walked over to his laptop and plugged in the flash drive that had all the information he took from the CIA. Documents and classified files began to blow up the screen. First, he ran through all of the documents and came upon one in particular, OPERATION: SIEGE. *Damn, all blacked out.*

Irritated, Fields started to scroll through data profiles on agents and personnel. He bookmarked a few and removed all the rest. He looked through the ones he book marked and found Agent Kathryn Madison, Active Agent for a year and a half, impressive record, and many accommodations. One of the best in her class from Yale graduated with a 3.9 GPA. Best shot at the academy and projected to be a top agent within a few years. *Interesting, I could definitely use her talents.*

He set her résumé aside and began looking for the address of a specific man that needed to be taken care of. After all, it had been two years since they last spoke, and Jacob needed answers.

Chapter Five: Jacob Fields

Langley, Virginia CIA Headquarters

June 16

Forty-five people sat in a conference room in H.Q., all waiting for Deputy Director Abrams to show up. Madison, still clutching her gut, wanted to be present even though she was supposed to be on medical leave for the next two weeks. Harrison sat next to her, impatiently tapping his foot.

Madison stomped on it, annoyed "Would you please stop that incessant tapping!"

Harrison was frustrated, "I can't help it, we finally have an I.D. on this guy who kicked my ass and yours, not to mention successfully infiltrated one of the most secure buildings in the world. Plus, the man who's got his I.D. is late." He started his foot tapping again, "So I'm sorry if I'm a tad bit impatient."

As Harrison was talking, a tall and balding man stepped into the front of the room and onto the podium. He started to speak, "Apologies for my tardiness, I was delayed." He took off his glasses, cleaned them off, and put them back on. He took a long inward breath before he started to speak.

"Okay people let's get started." He took a remote and hit the power button. An image of the man who infiltrated H.Q. appeared on the big screen, "This is the man who gained access to our building."

Abrams took another long draught of air. "This man, as some of you may or may not know, is Jacob Fields." There was a collective gasp and small chatter as his name was mentioned.

Even Madison was taken aback by that name. She knew who Jacob Fields was; one of the best agents to ever hit the field. She had read up on him during her training years and about all of the impressive deeds he has accomplished. The man was practically a legend within the agency, well was anyway. *Wait, isn't he dead?* She immediately raised her hand.

"Operative Madison, you have a question?" Abrams asked with his eyebrow raised.

Madison stood, "Sir, how can this be Agent Fields, he died two years ago."

Abrams scratched his head taking his time to respond. "Well the circumstances appear to be different. I can only guess as to why he has come back and why he attacked us. We still do not know what he was doing here or what he took." Madison took a seat and noticed that Abrams drew in his breath again as if he were scared himself.

"The last known operation and location that Fields participated was in Moscow, Russia. We had Intel that there was an asset that had information on nuclear weapons possessed by terrorists. Fields and Sampson were sent in to investigate, retrieve the package, and bring him back here." Abrams pulled up a stool and sat. "Jacob discovered that there was no asset and instead there was a bomb where this terrorist informant was supposed to be. As we all know, the bomb detonated, killing fifteen Russian civilians, Jacob, and injuring another two hundred. Jacob had stayed behind to defuse the bomb and failed. His partner, Sampson, was nearby but not harmed by the explosion."

Abrams hit the remote to move to the next slide. The picture showed a massive smoke pillar and flames everywhere. It was in downtown Moscow, a huge population center. "The explosion caused the Russians to think that the United States had just bombed their civilians, raising tensions that hadn't been that high since the Cuban Missile Crisis. Of course, tensions have subsided slightly since the accident two years ago, but they still remain high and the Russians still blame us for the bombing. This peace between our nations is fragile to say the least."

The pictures moved on and showed Jacob Fields again. Madison studied the picture with her blue eyes; Jacob was in Desert Marine gear hefting a SCAR and with Sampson. She surmised that the two were long-term friends, *but why kill him?*

"As some of you may know," Abrams continued, "Agent Fields was a former Special Operations Operative, or Navy Seal. He was one of the youngest Marines to be selected into the Seals at the age of twenty. He spent three years with them, undergoing some of the most dangerous operations in history. He was always successful in his missions. He joined the CIA as a covert operative for the next three years, along with his good friend Sampson here." Abrams pointed to the screen as he mentioned Sampson.

"It has become clear and obvious that Fields did not die in the explosion, and the intelligence that we have gathered, as well as his recent actions, suggests that he may have even been the one who rigged the bomb to blow." Abrams gathered for what he was about to say next. He wiped off sweat from the top of his brow. "We are labeling Agent Fields as a traitor to the United States of America and a terrorist looking ignite a global nuclear war. Agent Fields is now a rogue agent and must be brought in. This is now priority number one. Do we all have an understanding?" He looked over the room and saw nodding heads, "Good, Let's bring him in people, dismissed."

Madison couldn't place her finger on it, but the Deputy seemed more nervous than usual. Did he really fear what Fields could do? She rose from her chair and went back to her desk. Harrison joined her there and they just sat, alone with their thoughts.

Harrison broke the silence, "Jacob Fields," he paused, "This is unbelievable. How are we going to track, quite possibly, the best agent of the CIA?" Madison gave him an angered look. Harrison smiled, "Okay, okay, the second best agent of the CIA."

She looked down at her hands, exhausted, "I can't believe he'd do something like this. I mean the man used to do such good. It's hard to believe he's gone rogue." Madison said the last words with much sadness. She had done reports about Fields, done research about him, and practically knew his whole operational life. This was difficult for her. She looked down then back up at Harrison, "I saw him Lloyd. I saw him and he just gave me a wink and a smile then walked on by." She waved her hands and arms about in gestures.

Harrison leaned closer to Madison attempting to relax her, "Hey now, none of us knew what the man looked like. It's for agents' safety. It's not your fault, none of us knew." Harrison gave her a light pat on the back. "He beat the hell out of me and put the other two in the emergency room where . . ." he looked caringly at Madison, "where you should have gone too. You had me worried Kate."

Madison removed Harrison's hand, trying as best she could to positively say, "I'm fine." She straightened herself painfully, her injuries still antagonized her. "Let's just find this guy okay?"

Harrison looked down, disappointed. "Okay," he said, "Where do we start?" He moved his swivel chair next to hers and they bumped.

Madison laughed and hit him on the shoulder, "Focus," she said steadily.

"You know that's the first time I've seen you smile in about two weeks." Harrison smiled; it was all he was trying to get her to do. "But anyway back to the matter at hand, let's find this guy."

Madison smiled saying, "My God, you'll be doing something productive for once."

Harrison looked back at her, "Don't get too excited we're partners remember?" He smiled as he said the last part.

"I can still kick your ass in a fight too, remember?" Madison remarked in a smart-alecky way. She began to type away on her computer, searching for any leads on Jacob Fields.

Chapter Six: A Friendly Visit

Langley, Virginia House of Deputy Director Abrams

Night June 21

Abrams opened the door to his house after another long day of work. It had been another day wasted looking for Jacob Fields; he was long gone the instant he left H.Q. Abrams walked into the kitchen and put away his keys, got a drink of water, and walked into the living room. Abrams paused for a moment and sighed, "I know you're there Fields."

A voice came from the corner of the room, "I see your senses haven't dulled in the two years I've been gone Director." Jacob emerged from the shadows holding a silenced Glock 42. He pointed with the gun to a chair; Abrams walked over and took a seat. Jacob took a seat on the couch across from him and began his interrogation with a shot to the knee of the Deputy Director. Abrams was immediately on the ground screaming and clutching his leg. "My questioning has started Mr. Abrams and I do not have time for your bullshit so, do not lie. . . ."

—~—

Madison woke with a start as her phone had been vibrating on and off for the last five minutes. She reached out for it and answered in a sleepy voice, "Madison."

"Well it's about damn time!" Harrison said on the other line.

Kate quickly responded, "Hey it's 6:30 in the morning! What is it?" Harrison hesitated. "Lloyd!"

"It's Abrams. He's dead." He said slowly. Madison became wide-eyed.

She asked in a steady voice, "Fields?"

His response came in a slow confirmation, "Yes. We need you here at Abrams' house."

"I'll be right there," she replied. She quickly took a shower and dressed, put on her holster, and checked her firearm. *Fully loaded and ready to go*, she thought. The CIA agent jumped in her car and sped towards Abrams's house. She found Harrison waiting for her as she hopped out of her car. "Where's the body?" she asked. Harrison simply nodded to go inside the house.

The scene that opened up before her was a gruesome sight. Abrams had one knee shot and fingernails pulled. His face was also beaten and bloodied. Kate put her hands over her mouth as the scene progressed. A bullet hole was right between his eyes. Shot at extremely close range. She studied the body and became infuriated. "Why?" she said at last. Lloyd just shook his head.

A commotion was coming from the front of the house, and in walked five men. Kate immediately recognized the one leading them. Joseph Ambrose was easily the tallest man among them, standing a full head taller than Kate. He had short brown hair and a hooked nose. His attitude was more or less, for no beating around the bush. He wanted the cold hard facts. His stride quickened as he approached Madison, his breath hot with anger.

"This is one of the most insulting and disgusting things I have ever seen during my time at the agency!" He looked around at the agents surrounding him. "We are supposed to be finding this man, not the other way around! Now we have a deputy director murdered in his own home and not a single trace of Fields!" With his last words he over turned a table. "This is our job ladies and gentlemen. This is what we do for a living and we are doing a pretty chicken shit job of doing it!" Madison's face reddened. This was an embarrassment for her.

Ambrose gathered himself, "From this moment forward I will be taking full control of this investigation and acting as Deputy Director. All operatives are to be on alert delta. This is no joke people. We are now all targets for this rogue agent. Everyone must be alert." He took in a deep breath, "Agent Madison, come with me."

Kate quickly ran over to Ambrose as he walked outside of Abrams's home. "Agent Madison, you are hereby put into second command of this investigation. You answer to me and to me alone. Pick two other agents you trust to help you. We have no idea if Fields has his own spies within the agency and I am beginning to suspect a mole."

Her body shivered at the thought of a mole in the C.I.A. "Sir, do you really think Fields could have placed a mole within our organization?"

The tall man stopped and looked sharply at her, "Madison, if you even knew half the things I know about Mr. Fields you wouldn't need to ask me that question." He faced forward again and began to lay down the details. "Obviously, Abrams was tortured and interrogated. Even I am horrified at the atrocities that Fields has inflicted."

"Sir, if I can go back and look at the body . . ."

"No need." he interrupted, "Everything is being photographed and our techs are coming in to have it examined."

Madison paused confused as to what her next orders were. "What am I supposed to do then sir?"

"You, Operative Madison, are going to choose the two agents you trust and track Fields down." He finally turned to face her, "We have a single lead on Fields, security cameras caught sight of him heading south on 22nd street, Uptown Apartments. I want you to lead your team there, track him down and eliminate him."

Her mouth dropped, "You want me to kill Jacob Fields?" Madison asked astonishingly.

Ambrose glared at her, his eyes menacing, "I did not stutter agent. We have orders from the top."

Madison straightened herself, fully understanding his orders. However, something seemed odd about his behavior. He was tenser with that command than any other he had given that day. "He is not that dumb to let himself be seen by cameras. From what I've heard, he doesn't make mistakes."

The man didn't budge, "Do not let those embellished tales get the better of you agent Madison. He is on the run and is nervous, I'll take this chance that he did make a mistake."

"And if not?"

"And if not, I want you to find out why he did it intentionally. Either way, I expect you to apprehend this traitor." He glared once again at the woman in front of him. "Do you understand agent Madison?"

She drew in a deep breath, "Perfectly sir." She spun on her heels and walked briskly over to Harrison, "You're with me, now, you," she pointed to Lincoln, "You're with me too." Lincoln simply nodded and followed her lead, as did Harrison. They jumped into her car and sped quickly to Uptown Apartments.

Keith Lincoln was a fresh off the press agent and still learning the ropes of things. *What better way than to chase down one of the most dangerous men in the world?* He was of medium build and height, brown hair and brown eyes. Hopefully he would be keen enough to keep up with the other two agents in the car.

"We're crazy for doing this. You know that right?" Lincoln said from the back seat.

Madison gave him a look from the rear view mirror that stunned him, "The only thing that is crazy right now is that our boss is dead; killed by a man who was once a loyal agent to his country." She raised her voice, "And now we've been tasked with killing the most skilled agent in the world. That's what is crazy, Lincoln!"

Lincoln was taken aback by her sudden outburst, and sat back into his seat. Harrison spoke next, "he has to be expecting us."

Her eyes darted, thinking of a plan to infiltrate the building. Harrison spoke again, "Yeah, I don't like flying blind into this Kate." The apartment complex rapidly approached.

"What other choice do we have? We search the building floor by floor. Be careful not to spring any nasty little surprises." Lincoln tapped her on the shoulder and pointed to the apartment building, "I don't think we need to worry about doing all that."

Fields was climbing down the fire escape at a fast pace, and saw that their car was coming. He gave the briefest of smiles; they had gotten there sooner than he anticipated. He jumped down the remaining stairs and ran for it.

Lincoln jumped out of Kate's moving SUV and ran after him. Harrison yelled, "Go around we can cut him off!" Already switching the car into reverse to head back to the road, Kate was in motion. She maneuvered the car and sped to the back of the apartment building.

She saw Fields slip into a red Camaro and sped off with the wheels kicking off smoke. "Go, go, go!" Harrison screamed. Madison slammed her foot on the accelerator and jerked the SUV into a hard right chasing after Jacob.

Jacob floored his own car picking up speed. In an effort to lose his tail he swerved into oncoming traffic, and drifted into an alley. Madison followed him, and lost sight. She slowly advanced her car forward looking for any traps. Then off to her right the Camaro's brights flashed her and Fields honked the horn several times, making her jump in surprise.

Fields slammed his car into hers and twisted her sideways. He scraped by her and accelerated back out of the alley. "Madison, go!" Harrison yelled. She shook her head and put her foot on the accelerator again. Her car shot out of the alley, she turned left, and followed the red car.

Harrison rolled down the window, took out his Glock from its holster, and fired off a few rounds. The back seat window of the Camaro shattered under the gunfire. Jacob turned hard left and slowed down. Madison came up on his right and Harrison looked straight at Jacob with his smoking gun in hand. Right before he could shoot, Fields slammed on the brakes. Harrison fired and it was a clean miss.

Fields accelerated again, came up on Madison's right side, and slammed into her, making her fall behind. Jacob twisted and turned around several corners and headed for the interstate, Madison closely following him. He was jerking every which way he knew how and drifting left and right. Madison's car was accelerating too fast as she tried to drift with him. Her car lost its friction holding and slid into a pole and killed the engine.

"No, no, no, no!" Madison screamed. Harrison slammed his hands on the panel in front of him as Kate hit hers on the steering wheel. She tried to turn the engine over and start the car again, to no avail.

Fields slammed his foot on the gas and left them in the dust. He was smiling slightly. He hoped that everything he left behind in the apartment was enough to get the smart girl thinking.

Madison shook her head and tried to recover from the headache that again resurfaced. Harrison was outside of the car saying all the swear words that he could remember. Then someone came on the radio, "Madison, you get him?"

Angrily she replied, "No, he got away. What is it Lincoln?"

"I think you need to come back to the apartments."

Madison looked up at Harrison, "We'll be right there."

Back at the apartment, CIA agents were swarming the place. Bomb squad was deployed to search for traps. Madison walked in to Fields' room and was welcomed by Ambrose who ranted a stream of insults, one of which included "incompetent". That did not make Madison overly happy. She wanted, at that point, to punch him across the jaw. After all, what did he do to help? She restrained herself, just clenched her fists by her side, and apologized, no matter how much that bruised her pride.

She approached Lincoln, "Alright, what did we need to see?" He merely pointed to the closed door. Madison walked in and a string rapidly approached her face. Her reflexes kicked in as she jerked back. She blushed and Harrison laughed, "Watch out for those strings, they're deadly." He gave her a wink as he finished his sentence. She elbowed him in the gut.

"Lincoln? What is all this?" Madison asked as she looked around the room.

Lincoln replied, "Exactly what I hoped you would tell me, Boss," Kate surveyed the room. Dozens of strings tied from newspapers to other newspapers. "An order of events maybe?"

"Maybe," she said.

Her eyes converged on a single spot, pictures of CIA agents. At the very top was a question mark, and below that were two pictures, one of Abrams, the other of Ambrose. Below Abrams, was Blake Sampson and Jacob; below Ambrose, herself and Harrison.

Harrison's head was circled and a string ran from his picture to several other strings, then connecting to newspaper articles. Some of the strings included Fields, Sampson, and Harrison. All of the strings, however, led to the question mark.

Kate raised her voice, "Harrison, why is your picture on here, and why are there strings attached to yours and not mine?"

"Don't ask me, I'm not the one who put it up on the damn wall," came his angry reply. Madison's picture didn't have any strings attached. An inquisitive look formed on her face as to why the others did, but not her.

Strings were going to several different places, each one going to major assassinations or crises in the past several years. All of the strings converged on the picture of a question mark. "What are you up to Fields?" Madison said aloud. As soon as the words left her mouth the apartment's lone phone rang.

Every agent in the room flinched and pointed their guns toward the unexpected sound. Harrison silently laughed to himself. Madison nudged him while every other agent looked to each other, waiting for someone to answer; wondering if they should answer. Kate reached out and picked up the phone.

She put the phone to her ear, "Fields?"

Jacob answered, "Hello, Agent Madison. Thanks for the little game of tag through the streets of Langley." Madison felt her anger surge inside her, waiting to burst. "I expect that I have been put on speaker by now."

"You are Fields," Kate said through clenched teeth.

Jacob laughed on the other side of the phone, "Better luck next time." And the call ended. Madison, in her fury, chucked the phone across the room and splintered it.

Ambrose strode over to her and in a commanding voice said, "Agent Madison! It appears I was mistaken when I appointed you to lead agent on this case only just a few hours ago. Due to your incompetence we have lost the world's most dangerous criminal."

She tried to defend herself, "Sir! If you would give me another chan . . ." but she was cut off by the anger of Deputy Director Ambrose.

"You are hereby relieved of your duty effective immediately! You're lucky I don't fire you! I only give single shots in cases like this and you completely blew it!" He turned towards Lloyd, "Agent Harrison, you are now taking the lead on this investigation, are there any questions?" Harrison shook his head and remained silent, not wanting to provoke Ambrose's rage. "Good! You may remove yourself at any time now Ms. Madison."

That last stab hurt her deeply. Kate noticed he didn't call her agent at that point. She simply nodded, and held her anger in check. She exited the building with silent steps, took one look at her vehicle that she wrecked, and kicked it hard. The rim of the front left wheel came off. She knew she would have to place a requisition order for a new one, if Ambrose would even allow it.

She didn't bother hailing a taxi. She chose to take the long walk home and think about what would happen next.

—~—

The woman was lying in bed, tossing and turning, not being able to find the peace of mind required for sleep. The dark concealed the man who had entered the small apartment holding his silenced Beretta close to his hip. He stood there watching her toss and turn for a few minutes before going over to her cell phone and opening the case. He put something inside it, closed it, and went back to the base of the bed. He pulled a chair up and waited.

At long last, the woman opened up her eyes and saw a figure in front of her. Before she could scream, the man held up a gun showing that he was armed. She quickly shut her jaw, firmly.

"Now that we have an understanding," the man whispered. He turned on the light, revealing who he was.

Madison screamed. Her anger and confusion rising as she clenched her fists. She hurried to cover herself, as she was only in her underwear.

A smile grew on Jacob's face, "Now, now, did I tell you to move?"

"Kiss my ass, Fields," Madison replied and put the blankets on top of her. Her heart was still pounding, unclear why Fields was standing in her apartment. She spoke, her voice cracked with a small showing of fear, "Are you here to kill me?"

Laughing Fields pulled his chair closer to the bed, keeping his gun close at hand in case the nervous woman made any sudden moves. "Of course not, Agent Madison."

"Actually it's Ms. Madison now." Kate said with frustration.

Nodding Jacob replied, "So I've heard. You're still an agent to me, and that is what matters."

Her eyes squinted with confusion as her tone took a more angry turn, "So why are you here if not to kill me?"

Nodding his head, "I came to tell you that your life is in danger." He heard her chuckle a little, thinking the situation was kind of comical. He inclined his head, "Do you think I'm not serious Kate?"

"I think you're lying, Fields!"

Looking up towards the ceiling, Jacob sighed and rubbed his temples. "If I were lying, why would I go through the trouble of breaking in to this place?"

"Why do you do anything you do?" Madison smartly said.

"Clever, but if I told you, the men hunting me would bury me if they found my location or came forward with anything; including you." He looked down and his face showed what Kate noticed, seemed like despair. "I'm not running from the law, and I'm not running from a fight."

Kate took advantage of what sounded like solitude, "What men are hunting you Fields? If you are not running from the law, or fight, why are you in hiding?"

"Heh, you wouldn't believe me if I told you," he paused, taking a moment to choose his next words, "not yet anyway. You're a good Agent, Madison, and I need your help."

Madison's eyes opened very wide, in complete shock of what he had just asked, "Are you out of your mind!?" the sheets that had been covering her fell as she sat up. She got out of the bed and put on a t-shirt. She did see Fields tense up a bit and clench the gun a little tighter.

He chuckled to himself, "Quite possibly."

The room temperature seemed to cool as Madison's anger rose, "This is not funny!"

"Listen up!" Jacob's voice became suddenly very commanding. Madison was taken back a little. "I'm not playing games here. You're the only faithful agent that I can trust. Right now, it seems the people after me are keeping a close eye on you as well!"

Deep lines creased on Madison's forehead, trying to put all the pieces together, "Why would they be keeping a close eye on me?"

"Because you're the faithful agent; the good agent. Just like me," Jacob remarked slowly. "They'll watch you very closely now, because everything that has to do with me, and this investigation, could link to them. If you know them, which I do, they'll cover anything; any loose ends that they have." He drew in a deep breath, "I know you won't believe me, but I didn't kill Abrams."

Madison began to protest, but was immediately cut off, "I know what you're thinking, and I will tell you the truth. I did shoot him in the knee, and that was about it before he told me everything he knew, and, no, I won't tell you what he said." He looked at her in the eyes, "What I don't know is who killed him."

Madison couldn't help but ask, "If you don't know who, then why?"

"Probably to ascertain the information he gave me," Fields said.

Understanding the situation a slight bit clearer, Madison crossed her arms where she stood and looked toward her feet. She felt cold, but also was aware that there were some different things going on in the CIA. Ever since Jacob Fields resurfaced, almost everything she had known changed. Kathryn Madison was always one to trust her instincts and gut. Right now, it was telling her to put her trust in the man sitting across from her. She looked up with her crystal blue eyes, "What do I have to do?"

A smile appeared once again on Fields' face; he put his free hand into his pocket and took out a small piece of paper. Madison looked down, and saw a number on it. "Call me when you need me, Agent Madison." With that, Fields got up, and walked out of the apartment. Madison looked down at her hand one more time, unsure of what to do with what had transpired.

Chapter Seven: Safe House

Midday, June 24

Madison had her instructions from Fields. She decided against telling her colleagues and kept the information to herself. Something about Fields' situation and something in his voice told her not to tell anyone, including Harrison, about the late night chat she had at her home with Fields. She stood in her bedroom staring at her own cellphone. She started pacing around the bed, continuing to stare at it.

Finally, she reached for the phone; her mind made up, and dialed. The phone rang for what seemed like a lifetime, her heart racing because of her own actions. The other line picked up, "I said call when you need me Kate."

Rage built inside Madison, "Listen! I am betraying every impulse I have to listen to your nonsense and betraying my friends! So you better tell me very quickly why I should be listening to you!"

She recoiled from the phone when Jacob's anger spilled over to her side, "Listen? I'll be giving the orders here Kate! I'm the only one keeping you alive!"

"You keep saying that, but you won't even tell me who is endangering it!" She yelled into the phone.

Taking in a deep breath from the other side, "Because if I told you, you would never believe me," and the line went dead.

—∞—

Jacob Fields put his phone down and sat in a chair. Rubbing his temples and just struggling to breathe. He sighed to himself and toyed with the phone, thinking to himself, *who killed Abrams?* After Jacob shot him in the knee he started talking about everything he knew, but not who was in charge. Perhaps he feared the agent who was in charge of the mop up; afraid of what would happen if he revealed any information.

His thoughts drifted to Kate, *Agent Kathryn Madison... Good agent, easy on the eyes, and very good at her job. Smart and sophisticated . . . . Now all I have to do is keep her alive . . . .*

He opened up his laptop and began typing commands. A map came up and pinged Kate's cellphone, and hopefully her position as well. "Stay safe, Kate, and we might both just make it out of this situation alive."

—ɯ—

Madison stared at her phone once again. More questions raged through her head. Chief among them, who killed Deputy Director Abrams? *Just because Fields says he didn't do it, should I believe him?* She did. For some unbelievable unimaginable reason, she believed him.

If he didn't kill him, who did? And why would they? To cover up their tracks and to figure out what information Abrams leaked as Fields had said. It was at that point she realized that something big must have been going on around her, but what? Who was involved?

She considered picking up the phone again and calling back Fields, but he wouldn't help. He had his own struggles to deal with. Her heart quickened as a thought raced into her head. *I'm talking to and considering helping a known traitor to the United States of America.* She had to stop herself, quickly sat down, and looked around the room. Her breathing grew heavy. As she sat there quickly rethinking what she had done, her phone went off. Her hands were shaking as they went to her phone; Kate hit the answer button, "Madison."

Harrison was on the other line, "Hey we need you to come in today."

"Don't you recall? Ambrose didn't want to see me this week for my 'incompetence', remember? I'm off the case" Kate said with venom.

"Well apparently Ambrose changed his mind. He's calling everyone in today. Says he has a lead on Fields. I got him to change his mind, Kate. We need you here for this." Her eyes grew wide, did he know what happened?

She had to say something, "Madison. You there?" Harrison asked.

"Yeah, I'm here." She nervously said.

"Good! Get here as soon as possible."

Madison jumped into the new car she had to rent, an SUV nearly identical to what she lost in the car accident three days before. Ambrose wasn't nice enough to at least replace her car, let alone her pride. She raced to headquarters to find out what had transpired. Madison found Harrison expecting her in the parking lot. She eagerly asked, "Why have I been put back onto the case?"

Harrison grew a big smile on his face, "Seems that Ambrose has a need of the best agents, and you've been summoned." He slapped her gently on the shoulder, "I guess that means you and me too." His smile grew broader, "Ambrose says he has something that can trace Fields."

Her heart sank, "What exactly would that be?" Harrison just shrugged and beckoned her to follow him.

—∾—

Fields jumped into his car and followed the blinking light on his laptop which he placed on the passenger seat. Madison was back at CIA headquarters and he had to follow her. Fields had picked up a new car from a "friend". He parked his car down the street from where he saw Kate jump out of her black SUV. *Harrison, you bastard,* Jacob thought.

He hopped out of his car and went to the corner café to sit and wait for what would happen next; positive that something was going to happen.

—ꟿ—

As soon as Kate entered the building her training kicked in. She felt as though she were a target. Ambrose was there when she walked into her station.

"Ms. Madison, it appears that we need your skills to help us locate Mr. Fields," he said with a smug sentiment.

Kate put up an angry face, "Oh, so I'm no longer incompetent?" Ambrose fists clenched, but Madison just put up her hands. Representing she spoke out of turn, not wanting to fight. "What do you have?"

"You're a good problem solver, correct?" Ambrose questioned.

"In some regards, yes I believe I am sir." She replied smartly. "Why do you ask?"

Ambrose made a gesture with his head that implied 'follow me' and she complied. Her nerves were still on edge and her senses were very much heightened with the adrenaline rush spiking in her veins. *Could they know right now? Nothing seems different . . . . Just play along and act normal.*

They entered a room and it was identical to the room they found at Fields's apartment. The strings were going every which way and making no sense to anyone. "This is what I need from you, Agent Madison." Ambrose plainly said. Madison noticed that he finally called her *agent* again. "There are several things that we can learn here that could produce a lead, and I need you to find it." He pointed to the strings leading from each of the pictures, "Find out how any of these instances are even remotely connected to us." He made for the door, "Harrison convinced me to give you somewhat of a shot at redemption. I look forward to the results agent." With that, he left.

Madison breathed a sigh of relief. She was left alone inside the room to gather her thoughts. There was a computer in the far corner of the room. She looked at it, then put her hand in her pocket and took out her phone. She put the number in her phone to dial Fields and was about to hit the call button. She quickly put the phone away and sat down at the computer. Her hands trembling as she typed away on the keyboard, looking up the mysterious deaths, assassinations, and catastrophes.

She took out her phone one more time, having the urge to dial Fields rise once again. *Maybe he can make sense of all this and tell me what the connection is. He's the one who connected everything.* She put in the number again and hit the call button. Again her heart rate picked up again. The call connected, "Kate, why the phone call?"

She looked over her shoulder to make sure no one would surprise her. "I needed to talk to you again."

"Well I'm very flattered that a beautiful woman like you would want to talk to a fellow like me." He paused, "hm. Curious."

Her eyes narrowed, "What is?"

She heard him chuckle on the other side, "You're in CIA headquarters and you aren't tracing this phone call."

Kate became angry, and for an odd reason hurt, "Unlike you I'm not a traitor, and how the hell do you know that?"

Jacob laughed again, "I'm not the traitor here, beautiful. I am still a highly trained agent with my own way to find someone when I want to and know when I'm being traced. Why did you call?"

She hesitated for a long moment, "Why all the strings. I have been put in to a room to locate you!"

"So do your job and find me then," he responded. "Everything you see in that room is not meant to find me, Kate." She heard him breathe slowly. "I need you to find evidence that I was set up. I can't prove it because I don't have the resources, but I know I was set up."

Madison became upset, "Are you kidding me!? I'm talking to the most wanted man in the agency's history and you want me to get evidence to prove you're innocent!?" She drew in a sharp breath, "Are you out of your mind!? I know I must be. I have to be entirely crazy!"

Jacob attempted to calm her down, "Hey, hey! Calm down! This is why I left you the trail to follow. You, alone, are probably the only agent that isn't involved! I have clues as to what is going on, but as I said I don't have your database!" He heard her breathing fiercely on the other end. "Listen to me! I am innocent of all charges!"

"Why in God's name would I even believe you right now?" yelling at the phone and waving her fist in the air.

"Because there are some strange things going on at the CIA! Don't you feel it?" He pleaded with her.

She thought to herself for a moment. It was in the way most people were behaving. Abrams was extremely nervous, the eagerness she saw in Ambrose, and the killing intent in Harrison. She thought maybe that there was merely a bigger importance to this case than others since Fields was involved. *Could it really be that something was wrong at the CIA?* She lowered her voice, "Don't try to screw with me Fields or I swear I'll find you and bury you."

"I don't take those threats lightly Kate." Jacob said in a fiery voice, and the call ended.

"Shit!" Kate nearly screamed. She could hear her blood circulating through her ears, each heart beat being louder than the last. Her phone went off and an unknown number came up, Fields.

Slowly she picked up the phone and answered it. "Do not make that kind of threat again, or I will stop aiding in keeping you safe and sound." Her breathing slowed and she attempted to calm herself. "Are you calm now?"

Speaking at a reduced pace, "Yes, I'm calm. What do I need to do?"

"Finally! Thank you Kate." He said in a much happier tone. "There are connections between all of us because we were all either at those places or had something to do with them. I know for sure about that." Kate's heart dropped, she heard someone behind her open the door. Immediately she put down the phone and turned around to see a gun pointed directly at her head. The door closed.

"Easy there Kate," A familiar voice said.

Madison's hands went up, showing she was unarmed, "Harrison, what are you doing?"

"We bugged your room Kate." His voice suddenly turned angry, "How could you be working with Jacob!? He is the reason this nation is on high alert for another terrorist attack!"

The gun still pointed at her, she had nothing to say to her partner's actions, except defend her own, "Harrison something weird is going on here at the Agency. Don't you feel it? The answer is here somewhere and we just need to find it!" She waved her arms to all the images in the room. "Jacob left all of this behind for a reason. There has to be something here that tells us what the hell is going on!" Then something hit her, Fields had said that she was probably being watched, and now his warning was certain and her heart dropped.

Harrison took in a deep breath, "Why do you think I'm here Kate," his attitude taking a very serious and threatening turn to more intensity.

"What are you talking about Harrison?" Madison asked, her voice cracking with the unexpected fear.

His hands moved around the room, "Recognize where we are yet?" Harrison's eyes darting every which way. Hinting at to what was about to happen to her.

The realization hit Madison like a freight train. This room was sound proof, the interrogation room. No one would be able to hear his gun fire off any shots. "Yes Madison, we're in here by ourselves and no one will hear this," he tapped his other hand to his gun, "go off."

"But why?" she screamed, "Why would you do this, and what the hell is going on!?"

"You're in here to find out everything that Jacob knows, and right now it seems he knows nothing." Harrison laughed to himself. "And I thought he was 'the best'."

Madison's shock finally wearing off, felt her phone grow warmer. Her rage building, "Before you kill me at least tell me why Harrison?"

Harrison put up his head for a moment, pondering her proposal. "You see all these deaths and catastrophes Kate? We're behind it all!" He pointed to the wall with the pictures, "All of those people whose picture is on that wall. Everyone is connected to this," He pointed to all the other images. "I put in the recommendation to Ambrose to get you here. I put you in this room so that you could find where Fields is before he exposes us, or find out what he knows, and so I can kill you and end your investigation."

He waved his gun in front of her at a safe distance, "But imagine my surprise, when I learn you're working with him! Ha!" His head moved downward and he looked at the floor. "He has no idea either! So now, to cover up all loose ends, and to end your investigation," He pointed the gun back at the unarmed agent, "your life needs to end."

A voice came into her head, or maybe she heard it, "Throw the phone now Kate!" She grabbed her phone, now becoming hot to the touch, and threw it at agent Harrison as it exploded. Harrison shielded his eyes from the debris, and Madison rushed towards him in his vulnerable state. She tackled him and slammed him into the adjacent wall. Her ribs ached with the motion, as they were still bruised. Harrison's gun fell out of his hands with her surprise attack.

Momentarily dazed, Harrison shook his head and struck out with his fist and landed a blow into Madison's gut. She staggered back under the blow. She lashed out and knocked the flat of her palm in his temple and dazed him. Kate kicked out and struck Harrison high on his thigh causing him to buckle under his own weight.

Kate rushed for the door and ran out of the interrogation room. She sprinted toward the exit door, bulldozing everyone in her way to get out. She heard guards behind her telling her to stop. Gun shots popped off and she heard them wiz past her head. She heard Harrison behind her, "Shoot her!" She didn't dare look back for fear of seeing her own demise.

She darted out the exit and headed south. Not knowing where she was going, but running for fear of her life. Agents came outside and started to run after her and heavy gunfire was heard in Langley, Virginia.

—~—

Keeping a watchful eye on the laptop, Jacob Fields sat in a yellow Challenger. He moved back into the car after getting a cup of coffee. Kate hadn't moved in several minutes. The other blinking light that Jacob tracked, however, was moving closer. *Harri-*

son, Jacob thought menacingly. Harrison's dot stopped moving. The next thing Jacob felt was his phone vibrating.

He looked at it for a brief moment then answered, "Kate, why the phone call?"

Jacob barely heard her, "I needed to talk to you again," she said heavily.

Smiling a little because of his own wit, "Well I'm very flattered a beautiful woman like you would want to talk to a fellow like me." He typed a few commands into his computer, checking if his location was being traced. "Hm. Curious."

"What is?" she responded.

Jacob smiled a little more, "You're in CIA headquarters and you're not tracing this call."

Her reply was curt and unamused, "Unlike you I'm not a traitor," she paused, "and how the hell do you know that?" Jacob couldn't help but laugh at her last comment.

"I'm not the traitor here, beautiful. I am still a highly trained agent with my own way to find someone when I want and when I'm being traced." Now he had his own question, "Why did you call?

He heard Madison take a moment to gather herself, breathing in and out slowly, "Why all the strings? I have been put into a room to locate you!"

Jacob couldn't resist the opportunity, "So do your job and find me then." He heard her curse on the other line and then decided to take a turn for seriousness. "Everything you see in that room is not meant to find me, Kate." He drew in a deep breath, "I need you to find evidence that I was set up. I can't prove it because I don't have the resources, but I know I was set up!"

Kate came back with a vengeance, Jacob had to take his phone away from his ear under the ferocity of her anger, "Are you kidding me!? I'm talking to the most wanted man in the agency's history and you want me to get evidence to prove you're innocent!?" She stopped talking for a brief moment, but resumed her rampage, "Are you out of your mind!? I know I must be. I have to be entirely crazy!"

Fields had to do something to ease her rage, "Hey, hey! Calm down! This is why I left you the trail to follow. You, alone, are probably the only agent that isn't involved! I have clues as to what is going on, but, as I said, I don't have your database!" He waited, hoping to hear her breathe more calmly, but to no avail. "Listen to me! I am innocent of all charges!"

Her voice came back, "Why in God's name would I even believe you right now!?"

He attempted to calm her again, "Because there are some strange things going on at the CIA! Don't you feel it?"

There was a long pause on the other end. Finally she came back, "Don't try to screw with me Fields or I swear I'll find you and bury you."

Jacob was taken aback by her threat, and knew he may no longer have control over the situation. His only way was to use his intimidation factor again, "I don't take those threats lightly, Kate." He hit the end button on his phone.

Fields redialed her number, an angry woman answered, "Do not make that kind of threat again, or I will stop aiding in keep you safe and sound," he warned. He heard her breathing slow, "are you calm now?"

Her anger somewhat subsided, "Yes, I'm calm. What do I need to do?"

Jacob became elated, "Finally! Thank you Kate! There are connections between all of us because we were all either at those places or had something to do with them. I know for sure about that."

Then Jacob heard her drop the phone, heard her mention the name Harrison. His eyes flicked back to the laptop and the dots were practically on top of each other. Jacob typed in more commands on his laptop. He heard a gun click.

A few seconds ticked by before Jacob yelled into the phone, "Throw the phone now Kate!" He heard something grab the phone and the call went dead. The dot on his laptop that represented Kate Madison ceased to blink.

"Shit!" Fields yelled. He put the keys into the ignition and slammed on the gas and took a right. The wheels kicked up puffs of smoke and the street smelled of burning rubber. He took another right at the next intersection and then another at the next. He ended up at the front of the building.

Several agents were streaming out of the door after a red headed woman several yards ahead. He rolled down the window of his vehicle, took out his Beretta, and fired into the crowd of CIA agents. Pedestrians were running for cover at the sound of gunshots. Fields floored the gas pedal to accelerate to Madison's position. He rolled the car up onto the sidewalk and stopped just before he hit her.

"Get in the car! Let's go!" Fields yelled as he fired more bullets at the agents. They ducked in response to his returning gun shots and they fired their own. Madison took cover behind the vehicle and opened the door. Yelling louder than he did before, "Come on! Get your ass in here!" She climbed into the car and Fields put it back into motion.

The wheels turned and more smoke went into the air, Fields and Madison were gone with it. He sped towards the interstate, and by the time he got there, his police scanner was going off the charts. Police cars hit their sirens and were on the lookout for his car.

"Shit! Shit! Shit!" Fields shouted in frustration, he glanced at Kate and noticed that she was in shock. He noticed that she was clutching her left side. She'd been shot. "Damn it! Kate, hold on!"

Kate was slowly losing consciousness the last thing she saw was a police blockade in front and Jacob slamming his foot on the accelerator.

—w—

The room was warm and Madison could hear a television in the background. She opened her eyes and realized she was no longer in the passenger seat of Fields' car. She sat up, but immediately lay back down. Her left rib felt as if it was on fire and she put her hands to it. She lifted her shirt and saw a bloody bandage over it. Trying to become more aware of her surroundings, she looked around. It seemed as though she were in a small apartment, single bedroom by the looks of it. There was an open space to the kitchen that housed a small table with a trio of chairs. In this room was a single lamp. She was in a safe house.

Fields entered through the front door with bags in his hand and dropped them when he realized that Madison was trying to sit up. He ran to her side and helped lift her up, "Easy, easy. You have quite a nasty wound on your left side."

Kate's eyes glared at his, "Gee you think!?" She groaned in pain and lay back down.

"That's what you get for being a smartass." Jacob said, kind of amused at her comment.

"How did we get here?" she asked slowly, "Where is here?"

Walking over to the sink, Jacob poured a glass of water and gave it to her, "I have mad driving skills," he bragged. He pulled up a chair from the table and sat next to her "I avoided the entire blockade by turning sharp down an alley and evaded more cops along the way here, I switched cars halfway." He paused for a moment, "but I couldn't have done it without a little help."

Frustrated once again with Fields' vagueness, she tried to yell at him, but could not find the strength. "So you got me here and patched me up it seems." Fields nodded.

A knock came at the front door, and an alerted and adrenaline driven Fields cocked his head to it. He pulled a Glock from under his shirt and paced slowly to the door. He looked through the peep hole and saw that it was someone he had been expecting.

Kate couldn't see the door, but heard it open and two sets of footsteps. Fields rounded the corner first and the second person surprised Kate so much her jaw dropped and she was speechless.

Linda Baker smiled at her, "Hey Kate, glad to see you're still alive."

Chapter Eight: Traitors

CIA Headquarters

Midnight, June 25

Somberly walking into a dark room, Harrison carried his head down. He knew that the moment the door closed, he would be in for a chewing of his life. There was a single table, a single light, and one chair. He knew where to sit, and knew what was about to happen. He took a seat and waited for what was to come.

Several minutes ticked by, and Harrison barely moved. He was hardly breathing, keeping his eyes firmly forward. A screen came to life in front of him and a shadowy figure showed himself. Only the outline of a man was visible. He was clearly broad-shouldered and had short hair, but that was all Harrison could make out.

His voice was deep and dark, speaking calmly, but with a hidden malice beneath the exterior, "Agent Lloyd Harrison." A chill went down Lloyd's spine, having the man in front of him and just say his name, sent his nerves flying.

He wasn't about to show weakness, he looked up toward the monitor, "Yes sir?" he said with as strong a voice as he could muster.

The figure on the screen didn't shift and just remained silent. To Harrison it seemed like he was contemplating a punishment for him. At last he spoke, "You have failed to eliminate one of the better agents in the agency and could have single handedly ended this operation." Harrison looked down in shame, and could not bring himself to speak up. "Ever since Blake Sampson called it quits and then ended up dead, you have been my number one. You are the one to clean up the mess, if we ever leave even the tiniest bit." His voice became louder, more commanding, "Yet! Agent Harrison, your complete lack of skill has now left us vulnerable! But, there may be an opportunity here."

Harrison frowned at the comments from his superior, but held firm, "An opportunity? What could possibly be an opportunity at this point?"

Laughing, the shadow figure remarked, "Be careful of your tone Harrison. You are merely the tool which I use to carry out my will and you are rewarded by a very nice pay check. Do not forget who pays you." Harrison's jaw clenched. "Good, now as I was saying, we have an opportunity."

Taking in a deep breath before speaking, Harrison calmed himself, "Yes?"

Lloyd couldn't see it, but he felt as if the figure was smiling, "We have another contract, Harrison, one that can see us paid for quite some time."

Harrison choked up, "Sir, it has been two years since the last contract. Why do we have this one now?"

"You don't get to ask those kinds of questions Agent Harrison. As I've said, you're my instrument to play as I please." The figure paused and seemed to be glaring at Lloyd, making sure he understood, "I give you the name and you take him out, same as two years ago."

Harrison grew agitated, "Two years ago Blake Sampson pulled the trigger, not me. Not only did we fail, but he is now a thorn in our side."

"You know as well as I do Agent, that is not the full story! May I remind you as well, there are now two highly trained professional agents that are on our scent and it is all your fault! Consider this your shot at redemption! If you do not, prepare to be frightened of your own shadow for the rest of your life." The screen went black. Harrison felt another cold chill crawl down his spine.

Chapter Nine: The Genius and the Legend

Fields' Safe House

Early Morning, June 25th

Madison was in a painful rage, "Linda!? Are you freaking kidding me!? What the Hell!?" Kate tried to sit up, clutching her side and grinding her teeth. Linda didn't say a word and stayed in her corner of the apartment.

As soon as she sat up Jacob pushed her gently back down, "Easy killer, you got shot today and you need to lay the hell down." He lifted her shirt a little to see the wound. "Time for a new bandage." Jacob dug into one of the sacks that he had brought in and pulled out fresh bandages and a bottle of hard liquor. "Alright, this is going to burn like hell, are you ready?" Madison slowly nodded. Jacob pulled out a wash cloth and folded it over several times until he was satisfied. "Put this in your mouth so you don't break your teeth." He held it out and put it in Kate's mouth. "Alright, here we go." Jacob removed the old bandage to reveal a small 9mm hole in her body. The wound was still bleeding slowly. He opened the bottle and poured the liquid out onto the bullet hole. Madison's jaw clenched fiercely as the alcohol burned into her side. "That's it, that's it. Almost done." Jacob removed the wash cloth from her mouth and padded down the wound. He then put on the new bandage and pressed lightly to make sure the bandage was secure. Jacob inspected his work and was satisfied, "Good, all done."

Kate never took her eyes off of Linda, still in shock at her presence. She finally summoned the strength to speak, "So do either one of you mind telling me, what the hell is going on? You Linda! Why?"

Linda put on a smile, "Easy Kate, it's a long story." She pulled up a chair next to the bed and took a look at the wound. "Jacob has put you through hell in the time that he's known you."

"Heh, I'll say!" Madison's anger grew, "In the time that I've known him I've had two cracked ribs, suffered a mild concussion, wrecked my SUV, and now I've been shot!" She slammed her fist into the mattress, "Now, does anyone have the balls to tell me what the hell is going on!?"

Jacob put a hand on her shoulder and laid her back down. "Easy! You've been through a lot and there is a lot that you don't know." He waited for her breathing to slow, "I contacted Linda nearly a year ago. Maybe you remember the first attempted break in or 'security slip'."

Her eyes squinted together in confusion, attempting to understand the situation, "So what you're telling me is that you and Linda have been gathering Intel on the CIA for a whole year?"

"Two actually," Linda said cutting in, "and we have come no closer than you, unfortunately."

"So you haven't done anything to improve the situation in over two years!? Why the hell am I a part of this now?" Kate said through gritted teeth.

Taking a sip of water that he had pulled out of a bag, Fields continued, "Not entirely. We had a breakthrough and I found the location of Blake Sampson, my old partner."

"Why did you kill him Fields?" Kate asked.

Fields didn't bat an eye and continued to look at Madison, "Revenge more than anything, but he also had information locked away on that laptop of his. He had access codes to get into the main facility and server. I needed the names and files on several personnel over the past few years and what operations have been going on." He stopped to gather his breath and looked at Linda, "Linda and I have a history together. We joined the agency around the same time and we became fairly good friends. She was the one I contacted first. She helped me to obtain small bits and pieces of info in that break in a year ago, specifically on Blake Sampson. I needed to know where he lived. It took a year to piece together where he was. He always moved around as if he knew I could still be alive. He was right of course." Madison noticed something in Fields' eye, sadness, perhaps.

Fields was still talking, "After that it was easy to get into CIA headquarters and get more information. I obtained info on everyone, even you, which is why I recruited you."

Madison interrupted, "Recruited me? Linda, did you know it was Fields breaking in to headquarters?"

Linda responded to her question, "Yes, recruited Kate, just like he recruited me two years ago. No, I didn't know that he was the one who broke in. I was doing my job actually. Jacob knew that everyone who was not involved would eventually become a target, because everyone who is not involved can discover what is going on. Over the last two years agents, very good agents, have died 'in the line of duty' and no one was asking questions. Fields contacted me, telling me the same thing, and told me to wait for an opportunity."

Taking over the conversation Fields interrupted, "You took over the case, and immediately became a target, something I had not expected. I was thinking Harrison would and I had finally lured the traitors out. Instead you became a target. You would have eventually died under an usual circumstance and the blame would be put on me since they found out I was alive. If they didn't find that out, you would still have been a target. You're a good agent, and they cannot tolerate someone who digs too deep. So,

I tried to keep you safe. I'm sorry that you've suffered some," he pointed to her numerous bruises and cuts, "injuries along the way, but you're still breathing." Fields said with a laugh, "Don't forget you shot me Kate."

A smile seemed to appear on the hurt woman, "My only regret is that I missed," She shook her head, "but I suppose I should thank you for keeping me alive."

"Don't thank me yet, Kate. We're going to be all over the news tomorrow and labelled fugitives. I took the liberty in getting you some hair dye." Jacob took a few short breaths, "I do have some good news though."

Laying back on a pillow and looking up at the ceiling Kate responded, "What?"

Linda spoke up, "Fields put a small device in your phone that enabled me to hack into the CIA database. It was also a listening device and enabled him to give you an impromptu flashbang. I was able to hack even the stuff that's too classified for me. A week or so ago, Jacob contacted me after the break in. He admitted that it was him, though that didn't take too long for me to figure out. Anyway, he came across a file labelled 'Operation: Siege'."

"What's Operation Siege?" Kate questioned.

Stretching out his arms, Fields took the time to answer, "We're still not one hundred percent sure, but from what the two of us have gathered, the agency has conducted numerous assassinations and catastrophes. However, these have not been sanctioned through any of the conventional ways. The only question is why?"

Linda picked up, "We believe Operation Siege is a ploy to pit superpowers against one another and start a new world war. We don't know who is behind it and we don't know why someone would do it. The only logical explanation is that a terrorist cell has been built inside our organization and perhaps others as well."

"They use money to corrupt agents, keep them from talking, and use them to conduct these unsanctioned assassinations." Fields finished letting Kate absorb all of it.

From what Fields said, it made sense to her. She noticed something was extremely different when Fields had reemerged three weeks before. The agency had been on its toes, too willing to hunt down the unexplained. *How many were in on it though?* "Do we know how many are involved?" she asked at last.

"We don't, it could be as many as fifty or as few as ten." Linda replied. "What I would like to do is get access to everyone's financial account and see if we can find unusual amounts of money flowing into them. After all, a government job doesn't pay that well." she joked.

Kate was eager to know more. "So how do we find that out?"

Another boyish grin came to Fields' face, "I was hoping you would ask that. We have to lure one of them out, capture one of them and get him or her to talk and give us names. Then, we can track down who is getting the money and find out, maybe, who is in charge of the organization."

Understanding and nodding, Kate agreed, "Okay, okay." Creases formed on Kate's head, "I'm still a little confused as to how you two know each other, and why you went to Abrams?"

Fields put on another smile, "I went to see Abrams to confirm some information I had already assumed. That, and who was the head of the organization that he was involved in," Fields looked down, "though he didn't say. So after I had shot him in the knee, I patched it up and left the premise. As for how Linda and I know each other . . . ." He looked towards Linda.

Linda looked at the ground and Fields couldn't help, but smile. The realization hit Madison, "Oh my God, you two slept together!" Fields got up and walked briskly to the bathroom chuckling to himself.

"Only once Kate. Only once." Linda calmly replied.

From the bathroom both women heard Jacob yell, "If once means seven you'd be correct!" He poked out his head to give a wink. Linda picked up a pillow that Madison was laying on and threw it at him. Jacob quickly dodged it by moving his head back into the bathroom laughing loudly.

Kate couldn't help but laugh at the situation, clutching at her side with each chuckle, "Oh my God! This is so messed up!"

Linda looked down again, "This is not what I had expected."

Emerging from the bathroom Fields put everything back together, restoring seriousness to the conversation, "Now that we have that out of the way, is there anything else you would like to know?"

The injured woman turned to face Fields' with inquisitive eyes, "What happened two years ago?"

She saw his jaw clench, "It's a long story."

Chapter Ten: The Bomb

Downtown Moscow, Russia

June 9, 2013

The air was warm and the wind was picking up. Three men sat in a black van that was loaded with surveillance equipment. Fields knew his mission; retrieve the package, and bug out. He turned to his team, "Sampson, Harrison, you boys ready?" Fields quickly examined Harrison. He was brand new to the team and came highly recommended by Abrams. Jacob knew that this was going to be an easy grab and go mission. It would give ample opportunity to teach a new recruit the ropes of how typical operations went.

Sampson gave a wink in response to Fields question and turned toward Harrison. Taking in a long breath of air Harrison replied, "I'm good to go, Boss. I'll follow your lead."

Fields glanced back at his longtime friend, Sampson. They had joined the CIA together, and had gone through the Navy SEALS together as well. Sampson was a man he could count on should this be a cross.

Fields held out a fist in front of Sampson, and Sampson bumped it with a fist of his own. It was something the two had started doing before missions in the seals. Jacob turned his fist to the new recruit and motioned to do the same. Harrison awkwardly hit it back. Fields decided to give the poor guy some encouragement, "Easy kid, this is just a simple grab and leave mission. The bosses say you have great potential and that's why you're here learning from the best. Take pride in that." Harrison glanced up at Fields' remark. "There you go. I like to see some confidence."

He turned to face both team members, "Alright guys, you know the mission. There is a terrorist defector in the parking structure a couple blocks away from here. He contains valuable information regarding terrorist organizations. We grab him and we get away clean. I do not expect there to be any trouble, but then again, things rarely go according to plan. There could be men out looking for him. Be prepared for anything. Harrison, you're going to stay here in the van and get our link to the CIA up and running. Remember, Abrams is listening and watching. Sampson, you and I will be heading to the parking structure as though we are two business men. Harrison, as soon as you establish the link to headquarters, boot me and Sampson into the call. We have our earpieces."

Fields noticed something about Harrison's hand, it was shaking. He looked into Harrison's eyes and found them to be drowning in nervousness. "Hey! I need you to be one hundred percent! This is an easy job, we'll be fine! Get to it."

He popped open the back doors of the van and hopped out with Sampson at his heels. Fields slammed the doors closed and headed toward the parking garage with a big slap on the shoulder to Sampson. He turned toward his friend, "You okay? This is an easy thing."

Sampson replied in a slow manner, "I'm okay, just not enough coffee this morning." Fields grew skeptical. This is the man that held it together through some of the worst fighting in Afghanistan and Iraq. Why was he nervous now? He brushed the thought aside. *He could be under a lot of stress from the boys upstairs.* The pair continued on.

Fields hesitated before saying more, "So, remember how I told you last week that there was something strange occurring in the agency?"

A surprised look came from his friend, he simply nodded, "Yeah, about how all of our targets seem to be out of place."

"Precisely, something didn't add up. The orders didn't make sense," Fields paused again, "I told Abrams about it."

Sampson tripped and took a moment to regain his balance, "You did what?" He said with a degree of shock. "You don't have the evidence! Just a hunch! You shouldn't have done that without some proof."

Fields laughed, "Proof? What proof is there? All I have is my gut feeling that says we have been targeting random people and pose no threat to our country. They don't seem to be connected in anyway." Fields lifted his shoulders and let them fall, "I had to say something because it seemed too weird to me.

Sampson felt his chest fall, he knew that this would no longer be an easy operation or even a grab and go, it was an execution. He had done this type of mission before, fake a grab, kill the agent. It was the only way to keep the secrets hidden. He heard a buzzing in his ear, "This is Harrison, we're set up and the connection to headquarters is confirmed."

Another voice came into Sampson's head, "We're all good to go here." It was Abrams. Thinking that it wasn't possible, Sampson's heart fell a little bit more. "Sampson, you know what to do. There is no defector; you probably have already calculated this. There is, in fact, a bomb. We have a contract, and this is what needs to be done. Fields must go out with the bomb. As soon as you and Fields enter the building, you are to leave, and head for the rendezvous coordinates. Understood?"

Numbly responding, Sampson said, "Understood sir."

Fields looked back at Sampson, "Understood sir? I didn't ask you a question."

Sampson shivered as a cold chill ravaged his body. Fields slapped him on the shoulder, "Easy man I'm just screwing with you. I know you're nervous, but we'll be fine. I need you focused on this. Okay?" Sampson nodded again. "Have you gotten anything from your earpiece? I haven't gotten anything." Sampson shook his head. "Alright," Fields hesitated, "let's get out of this heat. The garage is right over here."

—~—

Harrison finished his secure link between HQ, himself, and Sampson. Feeling like he was gasping for air he opened the door and got out of the van. The city was ripe with life and busy people. Horns were being sounded at angry drivers and jay walkers were not giving a care in the world. This city took him back to his home city of New York, but he knew this would only be temporary bliss.

He moved back into the vehicle and heard Abrams finish giving orders to Sampson, knowing full well what they entailed. Abrams spoke directly to him now, "Harrison, you know what to do when they enter the structure, pick up Sampson, and bug out."

Biting his lower lip and contemplating what he was doing, he asked, "Should we be doing this sir?"

"Do not turn your back now. You're taking over a very special position and will be paid a lot of money to do it. Don't back down now. If you do; well we know how to take care of you." The warning was clear enough to Harrison. Get the job done and do it without asking questions.

"I understand sir. I'll retrieve the package and then proceed to rendezvous point Bravo." The communication piece was still active, but no one spoke a single word after. Harrison just listened to Sampson and Fields' conversation. Fields complained that no one could be patched in to HQ and that it would simply have to wait. Harrison looked down, *and there goes another good agent.* He moved towards the driver seat and turned on the van, pulling out into the traffic to pick up Sampson very shortly.

—⁓—

Entering the parking garage, Fields had a danger spike hit him. He knew when situations would hit a snag and this felt like one. Something was wrong. "Sampson I want you to be ready. Something doesn't feel right about this one. I want you to take the west staircase. Remember that the asset is on the fourth floor of the structure. I'll meet you on the other side."

With that, Fields slowly advanced up the staircase on the east side. Sampson made the motion to the west staircase until Fields was out of sight. He quietly left the parking garage and waited. He squatted down to the ground and put his hands on his head, and began to breathe very heavily. He watched as the black van pulled up with Harrison at the wheel.

Getting into the van, Sampson looked at Harrison with sorrow in his eyes, "Get us out of here Lloyd." Harrison hit the gas and sped away from the building.

Fields was heading up the stairs at a quicker pace, but as he approached the fourth floor he stopped. Taking in all the activity that was going on around him, he knew that was the problem. There wasn't any activity going on. It was as silent as the grave in the garage.

He advanced slowly taking short silent steps. He approached the center of the lot and when no one else appeared, he knew something was, very, wrong. Fields flatly said in his earpiece, "Sampson, you there?" He waited for a response, "Sampson?" Fields drew his Glock out from its holster, cocked back the hammer and stood in silence.

Fields looked around the structure and saw no one, just stationary cars. His danger senses were going off the charts. As he was looking around, he saw a small camera in the corner of a pillar. He moved towards it. Again he called into his earpiece, "Sampson!" but no response came.

As the camera grew closer his earpiece finally came to life, Abrams was on the horn, "Agent Fields." Jacob Froze.

"You have been asking a lot of questions recently and we just can't have that." Abrams stopped to ponder his next words, "It's time that we have an end to your quarries . . . permanently." Fields didn't wait for what was about to happen next. He darted towards the closest slit in the parking structure. A loud CRACK came from behind him as he sprinted towards the light.

As he reached it, he hopped onto the ledge and jumped with as much force as he could. The explosion's shock wave hit him and propelled him a little bit more. Jacob tucked his limbs in and flew into the adjacent buildings window and rolled, cutting himself on the shards of glass from the shattered window. He turned back to see the parking garage in flames and beginning to collapse. He heard the screams of terror from civilians below.

He looked up and saw numerous people looking at him. A police officer was in the office that he had flown into. The officer held out his gun and shouted in Russian to get down on the ground. Jacob feigned a move to his right and caught the officer off guard. He pushed forward and took the gun away from the policeman. Fields lashed out with his fist and broke the man's nose. He ran past the injured officer, down the flight of stairs, and onto the burning and dust filled streets.

—w—

Harrison parked the van five blocks away from the garage. He looked down at the detonator in between the two men. Then he looked back at Sampson. "So do you want to press it or should I?" Sampson took hold of the detonator and just held it. "Hey, I can do it if you don't want to." Sampson turned to Harrison with an angry look. Lloyd put up his hands. Sampson's eyes returned to the button.

Glaring at what the small button, he knew what it was about to unleash. He looked towards the building. Abrams had finished saying the key word. Sampson took a deep breath, squinted towards the parking garage and took one moment to hesitate before pressing the button.

A rumble came instantly and Sampson felt the ground shake. A pillar of flame exploded from the structure and a loud sonic boom hit the van. People began to scream and runaway, but not in time. The building began to collapse on top of them. Soon hundreds of voices were silenced over the sound of falling debris.

"Get us the hell out of here." Sampson said firmly, "I'm done with this shit." The van sped out of the area as military and rescue vehicles passed them.

—~—

Fields was limping now. He had landed awkwardly on the floor of the other building. He felt his back stinging with first and second degree burns. Looking for a way to get out of the area, he headed into the subway. He took out the damaged earpiece and threw it into the sewer. He also took off his gun holster and tossed it.

Jacob decided against going to the subway, he was too noticeable and looked for an alternate route. "Shit!" he exclaimed. Fields tried to walk faster, but he found his vision was soon fading. He heard the sound of police vehicles coming closer. Then he saw nothing, but blackness.

—~—

Waking in a cold sweat, Jacob found himself in a daze of confusion, *how long have I been out?* He heard the constant beeping of his heart on the monitor beside him. He was dressed in scrubs and realized his back felt like molten lava had been poured on it.

He tried to sit up, but a moment of shock went through his body when a hand reached out and grabbed him on the shoulder. He put his hand on the arm and pulled down. He came face to face with another man. Fields gasped in surprise, "Alexi!?"

The other man put his index finger to his lips and spoke Russian very softly, so that only the two of them could hear, "Easy my friend, I told them you were a Russian citizen injured by the explosion." He showed him an I.D. and passport that had Jacob's image, but the I.D.'s were Russian.

Fields responded in Alexi's native tongue, "Understood. What happened? How did you find me?" Alexi retreated from Fields and looked out of the doorway of the one bed hospital room.

Content that the hallway was secure, Alexi turned back to his friend, "Not here. Too many eyes and ears." Fields held out his arms and made the motion that said, "Where?" Alexi held up one hand and said, "Wait."

Laughing and hurting at the same time Fields replied, "What the hell else am I supposed to do?" Alexi smiled at his friend's humor.

A few moments passed and a hospital team came into the room. Alexi looked toward Fields, "They work for me. They will take you to a safe location. Do you trust me?"

Still speaking in perfect Russian, Fields smiled and said, "Da." *Yes.* The man who was dressed like a doctor grasped Fields firmly by the arm and took out a syringe. Not breaking eye contact, the man put the needle into the skin and administered the sedative. They waited a few moments until Jacob had succumbed to the will of the drug.

A few hours later Fields awoke in what seemed to be a small apartment. His hearing was coming back and he could make out the sounds of a soccer game being played on the television. Alexi rounded the corner and brought a bottle of water. He handed to Fields and he drank it gratefully.

He turned to face Alexi speaking in English, "Alexi, what happened?"

"I was hoping you would tell me, comrade." Alexi said, also speaking in English.

"There was supposedly a drop; a terrorist asset who defected to our side. Me and two others, Sampson, and a rookie Harrison, you know Sampson from back in the day, went into the parking garage, where the asset was supposed to be. Only he wasn't. I called out looking for Sampson and received no response. We couldn't get the communications up to talk to HQ, and when we did, I figured out why I was there. They tried to kill me." Fields said the last sentence with a ferocity that made Alexi take a step back.

Alexi nodded in response to his short synopsis. "I had hoped you were not behind the bombing of my people." He paused to consider his next words, "The way I found you was by taking a look at traffic cams shortly before the explosion. I saw you and Sampson walking into the building, and not long after that, Sampson practically ran back outside. He was picked up by a black van. Jacob looked down in disgust. His own friend, his best friend had betrayed him. "I know you're very mad right now, but you are in no condition to even walk."

Jacob slammed the back of his head onto the pillow he was laying on, "that son of a bitch!" He turned back to Alexi, "I need to find him!"

Alexi put his hand back on Fields' shoulder, "In time, in time. First, I need to know why they were trying to kill you."

Fields breathed a few hot, angry, breaths before talking. He needed to hit something. "I asked questions. I asked, what the purpose was in the last several missions we had been conducting, and they put me in a room with a damn bomb for an answer."

"And did you find out anything?" Alexi questioned.

Fields shook his head, "Not a damn thing. All I know is that my friends tried to kill me, and they are employed by our country, which is significant cause for alarm!"

Alexi nodded several times and asked, "So what can I do to help you my friend?"

Fields gazed towards the ceiling taking his time to think before answering Alexi's question. "Alexi?"

"Yes comrade?"

"I need to disappear."

—∾—

Present Day

Kate lay in her bed absorbing the words that poured from Fields' mouth. Whatever had been going on in the CIA had been going on for some time, and all of them were a part of it one way or another. A thought came into her mind, "Who is Alexi?"

Staring at the ground Jacob began to grin, "Alexi Romanov," he said simply. Madison waited for more information, but none came forth from Jacob's lips. She let out a long sigh and Fields looked up. Eyes meeting hers he began to speak once more, "Alexi Romanov is a KGB agent for the Russians."

Kate shot up from her laying position and groaned in pain, "A KGB agent!? Are you insane?"

Fields immediately laid her back down with a soft push of his hands, putting a finger to her lips. "Yes, a KGB agent. And the insanity plea still up for debate."

"How did you even become friends with one of them? They're the enemy." Kate said with firmness in her conviction and ignoring Jacob's audacious comment regarding his mental state.

"Well first of all, they are not the enemy. Before the tension between our two nations, which I might add was caused by our own; we were in the middle of doing operations with the Russians in Afghanistan." He waited for Kate to nod before continuing. Making sure she understood where things stand. He started again, "The Russians had a helicopter shot down in a small town called Bamyan. The KGB team survived the crash and SEAL team nine was sent in to retrieve them. ISIS had surrounded their crash site and was taking heavy fire all around them trying to hold back their onslaught. Alexi Romanov was the leading agent in charge after the previous one had been shot right after crashing."

"So you saved their lives?" Kate asked.

Jacob hesitated, "Not all of them. By the time my team arrived only four of the original eight had survived long enough for us to 'rescue' them. Alexi greeted me as you would expect, with malice and anger because I'm American."

"So you saved them, got them out of there, and you guys became friends?" Kate interrupted, thinking his tale had finished.

"Heh, not exactly, right when we punched a whole into the enemy's lines and got to the crash, more and more insurgents began to pop up." Jacob's hand begun to shake. "We blew up the helicopter so it and the technology it held, wouldn't fall into enemy hands, and fell back to a nearby building. Our ammunition was beginning to run low, and reinforcements were out of the question. So I had to call in for heavy, and I mean heavy, air and artillery support."

Raising an eyebrow, Kate questioned, "What defines heavy air and artillery support?"

"We had a battery of howitzers in the area as well as light and heavy gunships. We also had F-22 Raptors blow the shit out of several buildings." Fields stated everything with a grim sentiment. "In the process," he paused, and took in a sharp breath. Tears welled into his eyes, "in the process, a shell fell too closely to our position; it killed two of my men. Gordon and Chris were two of the toughest bastards I had the pleasure of working with, just gone in an instant."

"And Alexi?"

"Alexi was the one who took over after I was traumatized by the loss of two teammates. After the bombardment, a Black-hawk helicopter came in to extract us out of that godforsaken town. Alexi put his hand on my shoulder, claiming he couldn't have done that on his own or do what I had done. I had risked and spent lives to save theirs. He genuinely appreciated that, and from that moment on he called me brother and comrade-in-arms."

Linda interjected, "What was a KGB team doing there in the first place?"

Turning his gaze towards Linda, Jacob replied, "They were there to remove a high profile ISIS target. A man we code-named Phoenix."

"Were they able to accomplish their objective?" Kate asked.

Turning back to Madison, Jacob answered, "No, they were not able to accomplish their objective. Instead of Phoenix being present, it was an ambush set for the team. We have no idea how he knew we were coming, but he did. He nearly obliterated two of the best teams the world had to offer. After that battle, the CIA offered me and Sampson a position due to our impressive combat and operation record. We took it. I wanted it because I had seen everything in combat. I needed a change. Sampson took it because I did. He and I were great friends back then. Where one went, so did the other. As for Alexi, he and I participated in several co-op missions together to benefit our two nations, and became better and better friends."

"That explains a lot actually," Madison said satisfied. Jacob looked over to Linda to see her nodding in recognition as well.

"Anyway after the bomb in Moscow, Alexi helped me disappear and gave me a new identity to conduct my own mission. And now here we are after everything." Jacob finally finished his story.

Madison was the first to raise her voice, "So where is Alexi now? Could he able to help us?"

Shaking his head Jacob said, "No, he is not. I have already tried and he is dealing with his own problems within the KGB as well. He is trying to remain under the radar just as we are."

"Because of that incident we know, if we choose to believe you, that there is a terrorist or terrorist organization working through the CIA and possibly other agencies in other nations?" Kate said finally putting the pieces together. Jacob simply nodded. Madison put her hand to her face, "Holy shit . . . ." Again Jacob nodded.

Linda and Madison sighed in frustration, "So what do we do now?"

"Now, is the fun part, but we need you to heal first, Kate." Jacob said.

"And what will you and Baker do while I lay here in misery and pain?" Kate groaned.

"We used to have a saying in the SEALS, well for my team specifically. 'When options are low, go bold.'" Jacob said with a large grin.

Madison cocked an eyebrow, "And what does that mean for us?" Jacob simply winked in response.

Chapter Eleven: Capture

Midnight June, 26

"This is the most ridiculous plan I have ever been involved in," Madison remarked. She was still at the apartment with an earpiece inside her ear. She sat at the small table with two computer screens opened up to her. A green-night-vision screen was visible. One screen had the camera that was attached to Jacob, and the other was attached to Linda.

Linda sat in the back of Kate's rented SUV, nodding her head in recognition, "I agree. This is kind of ridiculous Jacob."

Fields was sitting in the front seat looking back at Linda, "Exactly. They won't be expecting this. At least, he won't." A smile grew on Fields' face, giving him his childlike grin. He was confident this plan was going to work, and if it did not, he wouldn't be around for the repercussions. "Kate, you remember what I told you should anything happen to us right?"

Her voice came back with an annoyed vibe, "Contact the email you gave me and send a message that says, 'Broken-Legion,' as we discussed an hour ago." She stopped talking to take in a few short breaths. "Who the hell is that going to anyway and what does that even mean?"

"Well, before you start to swear, I am fascinated by ancient Rome. They were sophisticat—" he was cut short by Madison.

"Don't give me a history lesson just give me an answer," she said annoyed.

Jacob came back, "Just send the message if anything goes wrong. Got it?"

"Got it," Madison finished.

Jacob turned back to face Linda one more time, "You ready? I know you've never been out in the field like this, but I need you." He saw her hands shaking and knew she was filled with nervousness. He patted her on the shoulder and held out his fist like he always did before a mission. He looked at her bright green eyes, "Bump it and let's do it." He gave her a comforting smile.

She attempted to return his smile and held out her fist as well and she felt his knuckles bump hers. He winked and jumped out of the SUV into the warm dark night.

The SUV was parked just across the street from the designated building. Linda had been able to steal several tech items from her lab before she had left to join Fields. Madison was observing the situation from the mounted cameras, hastily put onto the sides of the SUV to monitor any upcoming activity. She also had a micro camera put onto Jacobs black shirt.

Madison observed each screen carefully, making sure there was no one lurking in the shadows just in case there was an ambush being set up. Breathing slowly and attempting to concentrate she reached out to Fields, "No sign of street activity. Get ready to go on my mark."

Fields was just outside of the SUV waiting for his all clear signal to proceed to the house staring at him in the face. His hands were still and his pupils were isolated with concentration; ready for anything. Kate came back over the ear piece, "Go!"

Jacob darted across the street with all the speed and stealth that he could muster. It took him a few seconds to reach the house. It seemed the brick building was glaring at him. He sank close to the wall and became one with it. Trying to avoid any trip wires or sensors, he scanned the wall as he was moving towards his target; a closed window.

He had chosen this spot for two specific reasons. One, it had no screen behind it, and two, most break-ins occur at the front door and he knew that's where the security would be toughest.

Hugging the wall, he made his way towards the window, trying to be silent as the grave and to give no sudden movements. The window was close enough to touch and Fields felt around the glistening glass. He took out his utensils and inspected each tool carefully. Examining the window, he looked back to the tools to determine which would be the best option for the break-in.

He picked out the one with a hard, sharp edge. This blade would be sufficient to cut a hole in the window. Jacob began to cut the glass with his knife and the noise he made was loud enough to force Fields to stop. He listened for anything that might have heard the blade's edge. He didn't hear a sound, and he continued. With his circle cut finished, Jacob lightly poked at it until it became dislodged from the mother part of the window. The large glass circle fell noiselessly onto carpet.

Jacob let out a sigh of relief and probed his hand through the opening. Searching for the latch, Jacob kept making unwanted noises. He held his breath trying not to make more. At last he grasped the latch and pulled it up. The window pane was detached from the exterior brick wall. Gently he pulled the window out as far as he could, enough so that his body would be able to fit through the opening.

Satisfied the opening was enough, Jacob hauled himself up and through the open window. He looked down to make sure that he wouldn't land on the glass circle already on the ground. He tiptoed around it and threw it out the window when his entire self was securely in the room.

Jacob put his hands to his ear to activate his ear piece, "I'm in."

Madison, still sitting at the safe house, let out a long breath. She had been holding it in the entire time Fields had been outside. She put her hands to her head and looked down. *Don't screw up,* she kept thinking. "Great, now stay focused Fields," she said, in a reaffirming voice.

Whispering, he responded, "Aren't I always?" Kate could see it in her mind, him winking and giving his boyish smile.

Linda came through on her ear piece, "Enough small talk. You need to make it to his computer as we had originally planned and find out where Harrison gets his orders from." Looking over at her laptop and back to another screen that was receiving images from Fields, she was getting a lot more nervous. Her eyes kept switching from screen to screen. "Just get what we came here for and let's get out of here. I don't like being caught out in the open like this."

"Easy sweetheart, I'm on it." Jacob replied.

Linda became annoyed with his self-assured attitude, "Don't call me sweetheart!" She only heard Fields chuckle as a response.

Fields crept around the house in a silent walk, not wanting to trip any alarms. He rounded a corner and he appeared to be in a hallway. He slowly peered around the corner, looking for any signs of someone else being awake. He started to walk to the hallway turning; to his right was the first door. He stealthily opened it. Inside was Harrison, sound asleep in his bed.

A surge of anger went through Jacob, and a need for revenge almost overcame him. His breathing grew more intense, and Kate must have heard it, her voice came in clear through the ear piece, "Stay focused Fields, we're here for one thing. Get to it."

Jacob closed the door behind him before responding, "Roger that." He quietly stepped around the bed and searched for Harrison's computer. He squatted down to look underneath the bed and found what he was looking for. He whispered as silently as he could, "Found the target."

The response came immediately from Linda, "Now hurry and open it! Put in the flash drive I gave you so I can have direct access." Not waiting for Fields to respond, Linda was typing away on her computer.

"I'm going to the living room to open it up!" he murmured, not wanting the light to wake the sleeping traitor. He found a spot on the couch and opened it. The light blinded him momentarily and he cursed under his breath. He took out Linda's flash drive and shoved it into the USB port. A screen came up asking for a four-digit password. Jacob attempted to type in a few numbers, but the keyboard wasn't responding. "What the hell?"

"I've taken control Jacob. Sit back and let the genius take care of it," Linda said in an anxious voice.

Madison spoke next, "Let her do her thing Jacob, she knows what she's doing."

"That's not what worries me right now Kate," Jacob said softly. He watched the screen closely as the blanks were being filled by asterisks. The computer screen finally accepted the password.

Jacob heard Linda clap on the other end and muttered, "I'm a genius!"

Curiosity got the better of Madison, "What was his password?" Madison hadn't moved an inch since the beginning of the self-made mission. Her blue eyes firmly fixed onto the screens in front of her. She felt vulnerable in her state, and the bullet wound pained her dearly. Along with the other bruises she had, it wasn't a wonder that she couldn't have gone with the other two.

Linda laughed to herself, "It was his birthday, the self-assured asshole."

"How would you even remember his birthday?" Jacob said softly into the ear piece.

"I'm a genius, remember? I memorize a lot of things," she said with her own self-assuredness.

Madison couldn't miss the opportunity, "And you called him a self-assured asshole." She heard Jacob stutter a laugh on the other end.

"I wouldn't believe it if I hadn't heard it. Kathryn Madison actually has a sense of humor. Stop the presses!" Jacob laughed.

"Don't be a jerk. Where are we at Linda?"

Linda had been busy digging through Harrison's emails and wrapped around her work she missed the insult. "I'm sorry. What was that?"

"Where are we at?" Kate reiterated.

Linda responded with typing in the background. "Ah, well, I'm still digging through his emails and anything else that can lead us through to whoever is paying him."

Jacob asked a question next, "Are you finding anything useful or mysterious? I don't like staying in this house much longer." He could feel his heart beginning to pick up its pace, and could hear the blood rush through his ears.

"It's all encrypted." She replied in a shaky voice. "I'll need a moment!"

"Well you better take a little quicker than a moment!" Jacob nearly yelled back.

"Hey, I'm working on it! This is some heavy encryption stuff okay!?" Linda said annoyed. "And I don't like to be rushed! I'm not good at performing under pressure!"

Madison nearly yelled into her own ear piece, "Then how the hell did you make it into the CIA!?"

There was a pause on the other end until Linda finally responded, "Luck?"

Kate drew in a sharp breath, "Luck?"

Jacob came back, "I'll take it for now; just get us the details on the damn laptop!" Linda didn't respond and continued to type away on her computer. Jacob sat in silence, listening for Harrison to wake up at any moment. Adrenaline now coursed through his veins. The waiting became nearly unbearable.

Linda shouted, "I got something!" Another spike of adrenaline went through Fields.

"What do you have?" he eagerly asked.

"I have something in here that is titled 'Operation Siege'!" she exclaimed in excitement.

Madison took over the coms, "Fields, isn't that what you came across in your own findings?"

Jacob stared down at the laptop that was controlled by Linda, "Linda I need you to dig deep into everything that is associated with Operation Siege." His breathing became heavy as he tried to keep it under control. He started to think that maybe this had all been easy, *too easy*. "I want anything that remotely has to do with this document. Copy it onto Madison's drive. Send her all the information."

Jacob saw his computer dive through a wealth of information as Linda combed through it. Something caught him by surprise, "Wait, wait! Go back!" The images on the computer began to go in reverse until he found what he saw just a moment ago. "Right there, stop!" He couldn't make out the image entirely, "Baker I need you to clean up this image, it's too fuzzy."

"Already on it Jacob!" Right before Jacob's eyes the image began to clear. His breathing nearly stopped.

"Madison," he halted his words, unable to find them, "Are, a-are you seeing what we're seeing?"

Kate's voice also seemed numb, "Is that who I think it is?"

Linda began nodding uncontrollably, "that is exactly who you think it is. Who we all think it is. Know it is."

Jacob came in over the coms in a paralyzed, shocking voice, "That is the President of the United States . . . . And underneath him, the word, 'TARGET'."

Madison's shock overcame her, "Oh my God . . . . they're going to kill President Mathias Goodman."

Jacob's anger was now becoming apparent over the ear pieces and could not be controlled, "This is Operation Siege, or at least a piece of it! They want to ignite a war between Russia and the United States and the President is right in the crosshairs! I'll bet there is a similar plot in Russia! This is Operation Siege!"

"Holy shit!" Linda murmured. Her fingers now paralyzed in time and refused to budge.

"Linda I need you to copy those files!" Madison yelled.

Shaking her head to shake off the shock, Linda typed in commands to send a copy of the files back to Kate. She began to speak again, "Fields it's time for you to get the hell out of there."

"Right!" Jacob agreed. He closed the laptop and removed the flash drive. He rose from the couch and turned around only to confront Harrison.

His voice was calm and cold, "Hello Jacob. It's been awhile since we've seen each other face to face." Jacob noticed that his opponent's fists were starting to clench.

Fields stared at Harrison with hate, "Yes, it has been some time, hasn't it rookie?" Feeling his own fists clench, he lashed out in anger, a foolish mistake. Harrison stepped back and dodged the blow only to follow through with a cut to Field's kidney, making him stagger.

"Not a rookie it seems," Harrison remarked through clenched teeth. Lloyd reached out with his fist, hoping for it to collide with Jacob's skull only to be blocked. He raised his leg and kicked out. Jacob grabbed the leg and pulled. Harrison felt his other leg give out from underneath him and he fell backwards onto the ground. He rolled left, hoping to have Fields miss his head with his foot.

Harrison got back to his feet panting, "I thought they said you were the best?"

Fields smiled, "Heh, I thought we were just having a small sparring match." Jacob struck Harrison with a quick jab to his jaw. He followed by upper cuts to Lloyds exposed stomach. Harrison quickly recovered by kicking out and forcing Fields back on the defensive.

He put a hand to his cracked lip and stared at his blood, "Not bad Fields. You're still quick I'll give you that, but are you just as strong?" Harrison ran at Fields and tackled him to the ground. Fields fell onto his back and lifted his leg as Harrison came on top of him. With his foot firmly on his enemy's chest he kicked with all his might, sending Harrison flying into the glass table behind him.

Glass shards went everywhere. Harrison couldn't help but cut himself as he got up. "Not bad Jacob, not bad at all." He reached behind him and pulled out a Glock. "This, however, will be sure to put you into the ground for good!" He pulled back on the hammer.

Jacob felt for his own gun, only to find it missing. It was his own gun that was glaring him in the face. "I did have strict orders not to kill you, but I'm really tempted to disobey them!"

"Then do it! You better hope the first shot kills me, because if it doesn't, you'll be in a world of hell."

Harrison smiled, "As you wish!" He straightened his arm and drew in a sharp breath in preparation for the easy kill only to feel a sudden crash upon his head. Vase shards came crashing down over him and he blinked in surprise. His vision slowly faded and he crumpled onto the floor.

Fields looked up from his crouched position, "Nicely done Linda! Couldn't have done it better myself!" He rose from his squat and patted her on the shoulder.

"Is he dead?" She asked nervously.

Jacob bent down over the still body and put his fingers on the man's veins. "No. He still has a pulse." Linda let out a relieved sigh. Jacob picked up his gun and put it back in its place. "As much as I would like to kill him, he has the answers to some of our questions." He turned towards Linda, "Are you okay?"

Relieved, Linda replied, "I'm just glad I haven't killed anyone."

"And I'm relieved the two of you are still alive and I'm not by myself in this extremely mad quest!" Madison exclaimed over their ear pieces.

Jacob found humor in their situation, "And I thought you'd be glad to get rid of me."

"Not quite yet Fields."

Pointing towards Harrison's form, Jacob ordered Linda to turn on the lights and grab something to drink to calm her nerves. Jacob picked out zip ties from his pocket and set them onto the kitchen counter. "Linda, I need you to help me put his body in one of those chairs." He pointed to the chairs that had matched the glass table. They had bars for the backs, which is the ideal place to tie Harrison's hands and feet.

They set him down upon the chair, and Linda retrieved the zip ties. Jacob carefully put them on the prone man, expecting him to wake up at any second. When he was secure Fields stepped back to admire their handy work, "Good job, but I need you to get back into the car and keep an eye out. Linda nodded her head and took off out the door. She had broken it down to save Jacob.

Jacob pulled up his own chair and slapped Harrison's face. No response. He slapped it harder and more rapidly hoping to wake the sleeping agent. Harrison muttered something and his eyes started to open. "Fields?" He shook his head, attempting to clear his blurred vision. Lloyd's anger reached a tipping point as he realized he had been captured by Fields. "You son of a bitch! I'll kill you!" He struggled to get out of the chair only to find his hands tied to it.

"No need for swearing Lloyd. If anyone has the right to kill anyone, it's me." Jacob struck out with his fist, colliding with Harrison's stomach. Harrison gave a loud grunt in response. "I need to know who is behind your operation!" He lashed out again, "I need to know who is giving you the money!" He punched Lloyd once more, "Tell me everything you know!"

Harrison spat blood from his mouth. The edges seemed to form a smile, "You think that I'm going to tell you everything because of a few hard punches?"

A chill went through Lloyd as the man in front of him began to smile as well, "No Lloyd, I did not expect it to be that easy. In fact, I expected quite the opposite." Jacob pulled out his Glock, and tapped Harrison's knee with it. "You know, had you not killed Abrams, he wouldn't be walking well about now. You know what I did Lloyd. You were the first one on the scene. You saw him lying there on the ground, unable to move. It was an easy interrogation for you seeing that I already did most of the work. But was pulling his nails out and beating his face to a pulp really all that necessary?" Jacob tapped Harrison's knee again with the gun, "So tell me Harrison. Why should you enjoy the ability to ever walk again?"

An appalled look took over Harrison; he began to squirm under the imminent threat by Jacob. He attempted to move his leg away from the gun pointed at his knee, but the ties held them firm. His fear took over his need to survive, "Okay, okay! I'll talk! For the love of God, I'll talk!"

"Ah, now that's more like it Harrison!" Jacob's smile was broad now.

A voice came over the ear piece, "Were you really going to shoot him?" Madison questioned. Her anger had flared and wanted to see Harrison suffer.

Jacob replied, "Not here." He turned his attention back to Harrison, "It appears an associate of mine wants to see you in a lot of pain Lloyd. After all you did betray her, shoot her and ruin everything she stood for."

Harrison's eyes became wide, "Kate? She's still alive then?" He smiled again, "I wouldn't have thought you had a soft spot in you Jacob. My only regret is that I missed her head!" Jacob slammed his fist into his face, cracking his lips and dazing him.

Fury contorted Jacob's face, "This is no longer about Kate. This is about how we are going to stop you. Now, who do you work for? Tell me or a wheelchair will be the least of your worries."

Harrison returned Jacob's hard glare, "You already know him! Hell we all do!"

"Is it Ambrose?!" Jacob shouted.

Laughing as a response, "Of course not! He's too dedicated a man, like you, to even hint of betrayal. No, the man in charge is far more intimidating and will stop at nothing to achieve his goal!"

Jacob was now mere inches from Lloyd's face, "Who is it? Tell me! Or I swear to God, I'll kill you."

"You think killing me will give you the answers you want!? His agents scare me more than anything; his reach is beyond anything I have ever known!" Fear gripped Harrison, "Do you really want to know who's in charge?!"

"Speak!" Jacob yelled.

"It's the director of the CIA himself! Director James Andrews!" Harrison yelled back.

"Andrews?" Jacob said in shock, he grabbed Harrison by the throat, "Are you lying to me!?"

Glaring back at his adversary, Lloyd responded, "You hold the power of life and death over me, as well as my ability to walk! Why the hell would I lie!?"

Jacob had gone mad with rage, he couldn't contain it. He struck out at Harrison again and again. Finally, he yelled at him, "Why would Andrews do that!? He was appointed by President Goodman himself!"

Exasperated Lloyd said, "For the same reason I am, a very nice paycheck, plain and simple. Don't you get that yet?"

"Why the president? Why start a war between the U.S. and Russia?"

"Because that is what our employer wants! You think that your incident two years ago was only because you were asking questions?" He waited for Fields to respond, "No! We actually aimed to kill hundreds of people and to take you out in the process! You were the trigger man! The person to take the blame! We are getting very rich off of your misery and that of others! That and our employer just wishes to see the world burn! The biggest, most destructive terrorist event on the planet! World War Three!" Jacob punched Harrison again to shut him up.

He turned his back on Harrison, "Madison, Baker, are you two getting all of this?"

"I'm getting it Fields, still working on believing though." Madison said. She sat in the safe house, focusing on Fields' camera. She wished for nothing more than to be in front of Harrison and to deliver her own punches to Lloyd's face.

Linda came into Jacob's ear too, "I am receiving this as well, copying it down."

Madison turned to the other cameras on her screen and lost her breath. Several vehicles were approaching Harrison's house. "Guys you have company! Get out of there!"

An alarmed look overcame Jacob, "Linda did you get that?"

"I got it!" she yelled. He could hear her pant as nerves turned to fear.

Harrison started laughing, "Didn't you ever once stop to think why it was so easy to break in here? The moment you and Baker stormed in here, it sent a signal to my friends. You two won't make it out of here, not alive anyway." Jacob balled his hands into a fist and slammed Harrison's temple to knock him out.

"Linda get out of here!" He ran for the back door, but heard no response from Linda. "Linda!?" He ran out of the door and came to a halt with an M16 in his face. He ducked underneath it and kicked out. He landed his foot on the enemy's pelvis and broke it. He heard the loud snap and the cry of agony in the man's voice. Jacob picked up the gun and leveled it to bear down on the next person in his way.

He heard gun shots and knew from years of training to collapse and lay down on the ground. Jacob pointed his gun towards the sound of the gunfire and shot off a few rounds from the M16. He heard a shout of pain in the distance, knowing that he had only gotten a lucky shot. He moved into a crouched position and looked towards the shed in the backyard. He looked left, then right, and then dashed for it. Jacob rounded the corner as bullets reached his last position.

Jacob peaked around the corner and fired a few more rounds where there had been flashes of gunfire. Jacob only had a few more rounds left in the mag. He decided it was best to wait for his targets to appear in the moonlight. Three of them stepped into the small shimmer of light available to Fields. He squatted down to reduce his chances of being seen. He let off a trio of shots and the three men went down in a crash of screams and agony.

Fields charged back across the backyard straight into the house. He leapt around the corner poised to strike only to see three more guns aimed at his head. He heard the sound of clapping behind him. He turned around and saw the man.

He was the man behind everything, the man who controlled the CIA. The man was Director James Andrews himself. "Very impressive agent Fields. Very impressive."

Andrews approached the entrapped Fields, "You have been a constant thorn in my side since the beginning. Above all things agent Fields, you have been persistent. Now I have deeper troubles because of you."

Jacob laughed, "More troubles, eh? I guess I've been doing my job then!" He held his gun firmly in his hands ready to strike at anyone who approached him.

"Oh put that away you fool. I have no intention of killing you." Andrews said in a firm voice. "Besides, I have something you want, and you have something I need." He looked towards the front door, "Bring her in."

Two armed personnel came through the front door, in between them was Linda. She had been knocked unconscious and blood was streaming from her forehead. "Let her go!" Jacob yelled.

"Ah, yes, I thought that would get your temper flaring." He gestured for him to put his weapon down and Jacob complied. "There's a good boy." Two men were on him as soon as he had put down his gun. He was forced to the ground and had his hands were tied. "You boys know where to take him." He looked towards the unconscious woman, "bring her as well."

Andrews looked at Fields one last time before he was hauled away, "Yes agent Fields, this was all a set up to lure you out of hiding, but you're still a thorn, and you have answers I need." He looked back to the armed men holding him, "Sedate him and keep them both alive." With the shake of his head, "take them away."

—~—

Kathryn Madison sat and watched everything from her view screen. Her shock was barely wearing off. Her mind was slowly grasping at the situation. Then a voice came through in her head, *Broken-Legion.*

Madison turned quickly to her computer and typed in the given email and passphrase. When she was finally in she typed in the address where the message was going and typed, 'Broken-Legion'.

Madison painfully got up from her spot and paced around the safe house. Everything she had been told to prepare for had all come tumbling down. The rules of the game had changed, and she needed to change with it, or *be destroyed by it,* she thought to herself.

She waited for a response from the stranger she had messaged. Hours had ticked by and there was nothing. Kate closed her eyes to find some measure of peace. *How long would it be before they find me? Who can help me now? Who can help the world now?* Before long she was fast asleep, overcome by the day's events.

There was a sudden *bing* from her computer. She jolted upright into a fighting position and felt for her pistol out of reflex. She breathed slowly, focusing on the laptop. She opened her email and saw the stranger's response. It was only one word, 'acknowledged'. What would come next, Kate didn't know.

All she knew was that there must be a way to stop James Andrews and his gang of traitors, but how? She needed help. Kate prayed this wasn't the end of everything she knew. Faced with incredible odds, only rage and anger coursed through her now, and there was nothing she could do but wait.

World War was quickly approaching, and the only thing that stood between all-out war and peace was a group of rogues. Kate responded to the email for a meeting place. She was more than eager to meet the stranger who would help. Kate was no longer nervous, but ready for the battle to come.

Chapter Twelve: Interrogation

Somewhere in Washington D.C.

Night, June 27

His head went under the water again and again. His ears were ringing as the blood pounded through them, but he still never gave an inch. He refused to give up the information.

A voice called out to him as he rose from the ice, cold, water, "Just give us what we want Fields, and this can all be over."

Jacob looked up at Harrison and smiled, "If you'll excuse me Mr. Harrison, I believe I'd like to go for another dive." Harrison just gave a nod and Jacob's head went back underneath the freezing water. They held his head there for a longer period this time, hoping to get Fields to talk.

"Lift him up." Harrison said. Jacob rose from the liquid, this time panting for breath. His lungs burned from the cold water, but he wasn't about to tell them anything. "Jacob, just tell us where else you sent that information and where agent Kate Madison is. Then we can be done with this."

Fields started to laugh, "You can't kill me. Either way, you'll need me alive so that you can put the blame on me for the next assassination. So I won't give you the privilege of me cracking before it's all over."

Lloyd lashed out with his hand and smacked it across Jacob's face. "Tell us where you sent that information, or I can make your life unbearable. And I can do it with or without removing any limbs."

Jacob spat out blood that was in his mouth, "You have very soft hands Harrison, let me ask you, did you go to Bath and Body? I've been trying to find a new lotion and that felt pretty so-." Harrison punched him across the face with more force. Jacob spat out more blood, "Definitely Bath and Body." He looked up to Harrison with his boyish grin, "Is that coconut?"

Harrison started to laugh; he was quite amused and frustrated with the whole situation. He put his hands on his face and in anger punched Jacob again. Fields shook his head to clear it. His head was going to be throbbing for weeks to come. Jacob asked, "So where is our dear Director Andrews? Did he not wish to take part in the festivities?"

"The Director is interrogating the genius I believe. And if you know him like I do, you'd know he is far worse when it comes to interrogation."

A sneer grew on Jacob's face. He gazed with hatred at Lloyd, "Before this is over Harrison, I will kill you."

Harrison fought to keep a chill from going down his spine, but was unable as his body jerked. Fields looked at him with a malice that chilled him to his core, "We'll see about that Mr. Fields." Harrison lashed out once more to strike Fields. The impact nearly broke his hand. Jacob shook his head another time to remove his focus from the pain. "Jacob, just tell me what I want to know."

Jacob smiled again, "Getting frustrated Harrison? We're just getting started." He gave a wink, and then closed his eyes anticipating another blow.

Harrison raised his fist, but was interrupted by the sound of a door opening. Jacob looked up from his position and could clearly see Linda Baker through his bruised face. Behind her walked two more traitors and the Director.

They sat Linda down next to Jacob. Director Andrews walked in front of the two battered agents, "Well it seems you are both very resistant to interrogation techniques. However, this was only a warm up. It has been a long night and I require some sleep. Please discuss the matter between yourselves about how painfully each of you should die. Goodnight." Agents piled out of the room, taking their torture equipment, but leaving both Baker and Fields with their hands zip-tied behind their backs.

The door closed and Jacob fell on his back, "Are you okay Linda?"

Linda was still sitting up, but silent. She was looking towards the ground, mesmerized in her own thoughts. Jacob called out again, and she jolted with a shock, "Jacob?"

Jacob painfully grunted as he sat up, "It's me, it's me." He stared over to her, "Are you okay? What did they do to you?"

Tears welled up in her eyes, "The Director . . . he . . . he said that he would unleash his agents upon me. He said they would use rape as a means to get information." The tears began to flow freely, and Jacobs face contorted with anger he had never had. "They threw my head under ice water, and punched my stomach repeatedly." She paused to gasp for air, her breathing became panicked, "but I still didn't give them anything!" A light smile came to her lips and she shouted, "I still didn't give them anything!"

Jacob's face was even fiercer with her telling of what had transpired during her interrogation. The next day would be much worse. It would go from interrogation to down-right torture.

"You didn't give them Kate's location, did you?"

Linda looked down and shook her head for a response. The tears were dripping off of her cheeks.

Jacob's voice became firm, "Hey! Linda! We're going to make it out of here. I promise." He looked around for something he could use to break out of his zip-ties before switching to the last resort. He took in a deep breath and knew his only option was to dislocate both of his thumbs to squeeze through the constraints holding him.

With a grunt he rose to his feet and shuffled his hands until he heard two loud pops. His teeth clenched with the pain, but he continued as he compressed his hands closer upon themselves. Jacob's hands finally dislodged from the cuffs and he painfully put his thumbs back in place.

He turned towards Linda, "I need you to do the same thing Baker."

Sniffling she tried to inflict the damage onto herself, but could not find the courage to do it, fearing the pain. "Baker, if you don't do it, I'm going to have to."

"I can't do it!" She looked down in defeat. Jacob strode over to her and grasped her hands.

"This is going to hurt . . . a lot. Are you ready?" She gave a single nod. "On the count of three okay?" Once more she gave a nod. "One!" And Jacob dislocated both of her thumbs simultaneously. Linda squealed in pain as a response. Jacob removed her zip-ties quickly. "Okay now I'm going to put them back into place. Get ready." Without warning Fields pressed on the joints and moved Linda's thumbs back into their rightful place. Linda was gasping for air by the time it was all over.

Jacob heard a motion at the door and quickly signaled to Linda to get to the one side of the door while Fields moved to the other. A man was opening the door. The door opened in front of Linda concealing her. To the man's left, however, stood a very, angry Jacob. The man shook with surprise as Jacob wrapped his arm around the neck of the soon-to-be dead man. The agent was trying to yell for help, but could not. Jacob's arm was pushing down with all his might on the man's windpipe. Soon he was limp and dead. Fields gently laid him back with a soft thump.

"Linda I need you to stay close to me, do you understand?" Jacob's eyes burned with an intensity that Linda had never seen before.

"I understand Jacob," She replied through her tears.

Jacob lifted the shirt of the guard to find two pistols underneath it. "Do you know how to use one of these?"

Linda nodded her head as Jacob threw her one of the pistols. She cocked it back and was ready for what came next. Jacob looked back at her, "We need to stay as stealthy as possible. No gunshots unless fired upon. He closed the door of their former prison and walked out into another hallway. There was a door at the very far end. The pair slowly crept toward it. Jacob made a motion to open it, but someone outside put the door in motion. He pulled back on the hammer ready to shoot only to find another gun in his face.

Linda shouted in a mix of excitement and fear, "Lincoln!" Jacob and Lincoln put down their guns, both with questioning looks on their faces. "What are you doing here?"

Lincoln put on a large smile, "I'm here to rescue you! The two men outside have been taken care of."

"You're a friendly?" Jacob questioned, with his gun still cocked.

"I am indeed. You must be Fields. I'm Keith Lincoln. Don't worry; I'm on your side." He held up his hands after he put his gun back into his holster. "No need for that." Jacob stuffed his gun into the front of his pants.

"Where are we Lincoln?" Linda asked.

"We are at the naval shipyards off the Anacostia River in Washington D.C. You're in one of the shipping crates that the CIA uses for off-site interrogations."

Jacob nodded in satisfaction, "From here they could dump our bodies into the river and send us down the Potomac and straight into Chesapeake Bay; very well thought out."

"I am surprised you managed to escape," Lincoln said admirably, "I saw one of the guards outside head in there and I overheard the call that they were going to bring in a truck to take you two out of here."

Jacob raised the question that Linda had been begging to ask, "How the hell did you find us, and figure out that we are not traitors?"

"A story best suited when there isn't a truck full of more CIA agents arriving any second. Let's move!" Lincoln took the lead with Linda in the middle and Jacob taking up the rear. They moved single file between storage containers.

"I'd like to hear that story now please Keith," Linda begged.

"Really?" He watched his footing as he traveled, "Well, when agent Madison was accused of treason, I knew something had to be going wrong. So I did some digging. I found out that there were unusual amounts of money going to several agents, and when I mean several, I mean twenty to thirty agents; more if you count hired goons."

"Twenty to thirty!?" Jacob exclaimed.

Lincoln glared back at him and whispered as loudly as he could, "A little louder I don't think Baltimore heard you!"

Doors opened to either side of the small team, Jacob was the first to react. With quick reflexes he grabbed the arm of his closest victim and pulled him down. Lincoln made a similar motion on the other man who ambushed the team, kicking him high in the hamstring and bringing him down, screaming in pain.

Jacob still pulling his man, slammed him into the nearest cargo container. He lashed out with his fists, landing hits on the man's abdomen, but Jacob's attacker barely noticed the hit. The muscular man quickly landed a blow into Jacob's chest, sending him reeling back. The man charged at him like a raging bull before Fields could recover. He instinctively spun to his left and stuck out with his elbow, landing a blow on the man's spinal column. He staggered for a moment, but before he could gather his wits, Jacob took the man's head over his shoulder and pulled down, snapping his neck and killing him instantly.

Fields looked to his left and saw Lincoln still struggling with his enemy. Before Jacob could assist, Linda leapt onto the man and dragged him down to the ground in a ball of dust. Lincoln kicked out again, hitting the man squarely in the temple, killing him.

Fields, panting, "Is there . . . anyone else?" As he was speaking, three more men emerged holding M16 rifles.

Lincoln looked over, "You had to ask!" As he spoke Jacob and Lincoln went down into a crouch instantly and fired their guns towards the oncoming men. The loud gunshots echoed throughout the naval shipyard, but the three attackers went down.

"Damn! We have to move!" Jacob yelled, as he sprang into motion, pushing his friends forward.

"My car is just on the other side!" Lincoln said behind Jacob.

As the trio rounded the next corner of yet another cargo container, they ran into several armed personnel. All of whom were heavily armed and ready to take murderous measures.

Stepping out in front of the group were Harrison and Director Andrews.

Andrews started to clap, "Well done! Well done!" His clapping ceased, "I am quite impressed with your display Jacob! You killed two of my best men as if they were no better than novices! But I doubt you could handle this many Mr. Fields." He turned his head towards Keith, "As for you Mr. Lincoln, I was rather surprised that you were able to, not only discover the hidden funds, but also to locate the position of these two traitors to the United States of America."

Lincoln interrupted, "You're the traitor Andrews! I'll see you de-." A gunshot rang out. Lincoln looked down in astonishment. A hole had punched through his chest and his own blood leaked through. His eyes rolled up into his skull as he collapsed onto the ground.

Linda screamed at the sight of her dead friend, Jacob was frozen in his position.

Andrews smiled and reached out with his arm to put Harrison's gun down, "That's quite good enough agent Harrison, thank you. I think they get the point. You two are wanted by the CIA and by the United States government on the charge of treason; I am simply doing my duty."

"By torturing us? And killing the President of the United States is on you!" Linda was yelling with all the more rage from her recent torture by James Andrews.

"Well this job never did pay much Ms. Baker," He motioned for men to pick them up, "and the torture has only just begun."

Andrews turned towards his awaiting vehicle only to see it explode before his eyes. Before his men had any time to react, several more explosions went off around him. Gunshots began to ring out at the naval shipyard.

Jacob ducked for cover, grabbing Linda as he moved. They fell on the ground as the gun battle began to rage all around them.

Picking up his gun, Jacob fired at the remaining enemy still on the ground. He felt his weapon vibrate in his hand, but his ears were numb to the sounds of the projectiles flying around him.

He saw the man he was aiming at crumple to the ground. Jacob rose and lifted Linda up by the shoulder. Rushing for the cover of a cargo container, he gave covering fire for Linda to get to safety. She fell into a squat and began hugging her knees. Her face frozen with her eyes shut, trying to disappear from all the chaos and death surrounding her.

Finally, she grew the courage to yell, "Who are those guys!?"

Jacob smiled as he fired his weapon, "That's the cavalry!"

Kathryn Madison followed the Director's car earlier that morning to the docks near the Potomac River. Her newfound ally had given her the instructions, and she complied without complaint. She was furious with the recent events and the new information that came to light. She was ready to put as many traitors into the ground as it took.

She dialed her phone and waited for the other end to pick up, "I've got him. Naval Shipyard," and she hung up her phone.

Kate waited for her newfound ally's team at the edge of the docks. There were several cargo containers providing great ambush positions. They waited until it grew dark; the team needed it to move into position.

As darkness took over, the team moved into the docks. Madison, still in pain from her wound chose to take a spot on the ground level rather than taking to the tops of cargo containers.

They waited for the Director to reemerge from his torture session near the middle of the containers. He revealed himself in the limelight and took a group of five agents around him, including Harrison.

Madison's eyes grew bright at the prospect of revenge. She made a movement to pull back on the hammer, but a hand stopped her.

It was the stranger she had met, "Not yet," he said steadily with his accent.

She watched silently as Andrews and Harrison made their way back towards their vehicles, but suddenly more agents arrived. Two trucks carrying at least six men each. The group stopped to chat and idle away the time.

Kate tried to keep her anxiety in check. Inside her, a fire was brewing that wanted to take on all the men on her own. Only her training kept her grounded.

The man beside her whispered in her ear again, "Soon," as she let out her breath slowly.

Minutes turned to an hour as they stood still watching the traitors. Then she heard the sound of gunshots, taking her by surprise as well as the group in front of her. They ran towards their vehicles and grabbed their weapons.

She spoke into her earpiece before anyone had the chance to react, "Everyone hold your fire! We don't know what's happening yet!"

Three figures emerged from around a nearby corner; she recognized them as Fields, Linda, and to a huge surprise, Keith Lincoln. She held her breath as the conspirators turned to face their rivals.

Kate winced at the sound of Andrews clapping. He was commending them for their progress, and Lincoln stepped forward. He yelled back at Andrews. As he did Harrison raised his weapon.

Madison was about to scream at Lincoln to duck, but a hand covered her mouth before she could yell. Her new ally was trying to keep her silent so they could retain the element of surprise. With her mouth covered, her eyes bulged at the sight of Harrison shooting Lincoln.

The man covering her mouth removed his hand, "There was nothing you could do." He looked around him, "The team is in position, give the order."

Kate wiped away the single tear from her face before speaking again, "Now!"

The team sprang into action; three of the members held rocket launchers and sent the rockets into the vehicles, catching everyone by surprise. Andrews fell to the floor in terror as the ambush had begun.

"Fire at will!" Kate screamed into her ear piece, and gunshots from numerous teammates sounded. Chaos erupted throughout the traitors' ranks. Many of them ran for cover, but a few of the unlucky ones went down in the first salvo.

Madison lifted her own weapon and shot at the person with whom all her hatred laid, Lloyd Harrison.

Harrison crouched below her gunshots and returned fire with his Berretta. Madison took cover behind the corner of the cargo container as the bullets ricocheted off hard metal. She turned around and ran towards the other end to move at a flanking maneuver.

She ran into a man, but before he could react, his stomach was ripped open with several bullets. Madison's smoking gun took aim at another, but he ducked between the structures.

The remaining enemy agents fell back towards the last remaining defensible position. Andrews and Harrison were still among the living.

Pouring all the remaining bullets she had left in the magazine at Harrison's head, she failed to realize that Jacob and Linda had crept up behind her during the madness of the heated gun battle.

Jacob grabbed her shoulder, "Kate!"

Madison lurched around in surprise, and made a move to strike at Fields, but he caught her arm.

"Kate we need to get out of here! They have reinforcements coming any second now! We need to evacuate while we still have a chance!"

Madison took one last look at the agents in their desperate position, "We just need a little more time and we can end this here!"

Jacob shook his head angrily, "There isn't enough time to finish them! Pull everyone back!"

Grinding her teeth, Madison gave the order, "Everyone, evacuate the premises! Enemy reinforcements are on their way and we need to bug out!"

As the team members complied, the gunshots began to subside, and sirens began to roar.

"Get to the boats!"

Madison led Jacob and Linda to the nearest motor raft. Jet black, and near impossible to see at night. They climbed in, with the stranger and two other members of the team. They sped off into the night, only the motor making a sound.

Jacob turned around to face the group on the small raft, "Thanks for pulling my nuts out of the fire again Alexi."

Alexi Romanov gave his friend a large smile and a curt nod, "I still owe you several more comrade."

Chapter Thirteen: Death Sentence

Langley Virginia, CIA Headquarters

Day June 28

"How could you possibly be so damned stupid and foolish? How could you be a downright imbecile? How could you be a complete screw up, Agent Harrison?!"

Harrison looked down in shame, not wanting to risk the further tongue lashing from Director Andrews. His hair was standing up on his back and his heart was beating rapidly.

Andrews leaned in very close to his face, screaming into it, "I wish I could bring Sampson back from the dead and have him kill you then he can go back to his slumber! Then I could forget about the damned contract, and just make you face an unforgiving and extremely painful death! If there is a God Harrison, I swear to him, that if we fail in this next contract, I will have your head on a spike. Your insides will be ripped out, your eyes gouged out, and finally your tongue cut out!"

Harrison held his breath, not wanting to breathe out of fear that the Director will kill him for the simple process of living.

Andrews continued, "Jacob Fields, his team, and whatever else he had in play there are now right on our trail! We left the perfect bait! The perfect trap! We had him and you let him fly through your fingers! Your usefulness seems to be nearing its end!"

Harrison's heart beat faster than it had before. He felt as though he was going to have a heart attack, when suddenly the Director said something he wasn't expecting to hear.

"But, Lloyd Harrison."

Harrison looked up, hopeful that his executioner had not let the guillotine down yet, "Sir?"

Andrews fell back into his chair and motioned for Harrison to have a seat across from him. Harrison gladly took it. His eyes firmly locked onto the Director, waiting for the hope that was coming.

A smile came to Andrews and he started to laugh, "But Lloyd, I need you. You are the last best asset I have unfortunately, and I will let you live, rather than have his agents track you down and kill you."

"You would send his agents after me?" Harrison asked, shocked.

"You're damn right, and I will if we fail! You know what they are capable of. I will not tolerate your incompetence any longer. You fail once more, and your body shall never be seen again. Do you understand me?" Andrews' cold, hard, blue eyes, gazed through Harrison causing him to shiver with nervousness.

He nodded through his discomfort, "Perfectly sir."

"Now that we have that settled," Andrews pulled something out from his drawer, several satellite images from Fields escape, "Who are these new players in our game?"

Harrison sat forward, staring at the highlighted dots all around their team from the past night. He looked up, "Did Fields hire mercenaries?"

"Unlikely. We searched Fields from top to bottom, no trackers. We must have been followed. The only people that could have known we were involved are Fields, Baker, and Madison."

Harrison's eyes narrowed, "Madison, she wasn't with Fields as we predicted. Instead it was Baker; an unexpected turn. She may have contacted someone."

"But who would she know? No, this all holds its roots in Fields. I want to know who these new people are Harrison."

An agent walked in the room and interrupted the conversation between the two conspirators, "Sir, we've scanned everything from the area of your attack. Nothing, but the bullets of your assailants have been found. The rounds are from standard gang weapons in the surrounding area of Washington."

"What kind of weapons?" Andrews inquired.

"AK-47s and M16s."

Andrews dismissed the loyal agent, "Thank you Jones; that will be all."

Harrison cocked his head, "AK-47s and M16s? You don't think Fields got a gang to bail his ass out of the fire do you?"

"Not in the least. Their attack was too coordinated. In fact . . ." Andrews trailed off as he looked down towards the satellite images before him, "I've seen this maneuver before." He shifted the photos towards Harrison, "Anything look familiar to you, Harrison?"

He looked at the photos intently before noticing the complete obvious, "These are standard KGB ambush tactics! They've used them several times in Afghanistan, Syria, and several other countries! Fields has a KGB squad on his team!?"

"It would appear that way." Andrews' eyes darted from left to right thinking.

"Director, he's gaining more assets," Harrison pointed out.

"Thank you for stating the obvious, Lloyd Harrison. Now for the reason I called you in here." He turned his intense gaze back towards Harrison, "We are moving up our time table."

"We are?"

"Indeed. Recent events have shown that we cannot sit idly by while these loyalists destroy everything we've accomplished." He slammed his fist on the table, "Too damn far, Harrison! We have an opportunity on the thirtieth."

Harrison nearly leaped out of his chair in surprise, "That's only two days from now! How? We don't have a plan for any of this!"

"Hence why I called you in here, Harrison. We are going to put our heads together to come up with some ideas."

Harrison laughed, but refrained from relaxing, "Well for starters where is the president going to be on the thirtieth?"

"There is a speech that he is giving on the White House lawn. There will be thousands of people in the crowd, a perfect opportunity to blend in with the crowd." A smile touched the Director's lips, "And plenty of surrounding buildings for our high velocity guns to reach our target."

Harrison's eyes narrowed, "You want to use high velocity guns sir?"

"More specifically we need to use Russian high velocity guns with Russian slugs."

"That makes sense considering what our employer is attempting to accomplish." Harrison pointed out.

Andrews nodded his head, agreeing with Harrison's assessment of their employer's goals. He reached into his drawer and pulled out a box of cigarettes and offered one to Lloyd. He took it.

Both conspirators sat in silence, enjoying a smoke together envisioning the future to come. A realization came to Harrison and he turned to the Director.

"The agents we put in place will need to speak Russian. We need to make this look as if the Russians actually set this up. We need people who aren't afraid of getting caught." He drew in a breath before he continued, "We need to make this as believable as possible, sir. If we do not, it's all of our heads. Especially if an agent that gets captured is revealed to be one of ours."

Harrison noticed the director nodding his head throughout his collection of thoughts, "Indeed Harrison." He turned his head back to Lloyd, "Which is why there will be no teams, just a man to take the shot."

Harrison's eyes grew wide, "Just one man?"

Andrews nodded, "Just one."

"You want me to take the shot at the president, and then get caught?"

"By all means avoid capture at all costs, and we will have a fall man as we usually do." The Director's voice turned into a harsh growl, "However! Since you are truly the only man that can pull this off that is entirely loyal to me. I'd rather not take the risk of a stupid mercenary that we pay to screw it up. If you do, well, you already know what will happen. We've discussed that already."

Harrison gulped, "Yes sir."

"In the event that you do fail Mr. Harrison, we have standby teams to take out the target, but that will not stop me from carrying out my promise to you." The Directors eyes seemed to glare with hate towards Harrison.

The Director continued, "There is one small detail that we are forgetting."

"Sir?"

"Jacob Fields."

Harrison held up his chin, "Ah. Him. What do you think we should do about him? He has been a constant thorn in our side since the very beginning. Even when Abrams was in charge, he caused problems for everyone involved."

"Mr. Fields believes himself to be the righteous man. In fact, I think we have just found our fall man. We won't need to do anything for that as Mr. Fields has already fulfilled that role for us. Jacob Fields has already been shown to the entire country. He is wanted in every county of every state. If he and his team try to intervene, we have plenty of resources in place to take him out and make him out to be the bad guy in all of this."

"But what should we do about it?"

An idea came to the Director, "I'll put Joseph Ambrose on the task. He still believes Jacob, Linda, and Kate to be enemies of the state. He never questions orders."

Nodding in agreement Harrison asked another question, "And what of the KGB team at his disposal? They will be another beast to deal with."

"That is another factor we have yet to consider." The Director took another puff on his cigarette while he mulled over his thoughts, "There are several different variables that need to be taken care of. We do have one advantage over them."

"What is that Director?"

"They do not know when we will execute Operation Siege, but I have my guesses that they will catch on to that very soon now that they know the president is now our target."

Harrison raised his opinion, "They are not that great in number. They won't be able to find my perch in time to stop the shooting, and they won't be able to get close to the president with that many Secret Service guards."

The Director nodded again, agreeing with his conspirator, "Then on the thirtieth we kill our Commander in Chief."

Chapter Fourteen: The Plan

Fields' Safe House

Day, June 28

The small band of loyalists was gathered in the one bedroom safe house. Many of them were collected in the kitchen for a total of six, while the four people in charge sat around the table.

Kathryn Madison was still clutching the wound at her side, feeling the wound as it was finally beginning to heal. Across from her sat Jacob Fields, the legend of the CIA and Special Forces. Beside him sat the Genius, Linda Baker, still shaken up from her ordeal at the docks. Across from her sat Alexi Romanov, the leader of the best KGB team in Russia and the savior of the docks.

Jacob started their afternoon meeting, "Thank you once again Alexi. We wouldn't have made it out of there without you."

Alexi bowed his head humbly and replied, "Anything for you comrade. When your associate here messaged me your go to phrase, 'Broken-Legion' I knew that you had fallen into some serious shit." He laughed as he recollected every time the each other had used that phrase to bail the other out of the fire. "This wasn't our first time saving your ass nor will it be the last, I bet."

Jacob put on his boyish grin, "Most likely not, knowing how we both have a knack for falling into the fire in the first place."

Madison spoke up, "As fun as this is for reminiscing and remembering who saved whom, we need to discuss what our next move will be."

Linda was nodding her head in agreement as Jacob spoke, "Agreed! That is why we have finally all gathered here after our day of rest." His face was not as bruised as he once thought. His right cheek bone had the only evident bruise on his face at the time. Linda faired less. Her stomach was dotted with dozens of black and blue bruises. Then there was Alexi who had remained alert the entire night and day while they were in recovery. Madison's bullet wound had only just begun to heal. Jacob put a guess on the combat readiness of his group at seventy percent. Jacob's mind already put together that he would need Madison's and Baker's skills for the next few days, otherwise everything they had accomplished would be undone. As for Alexi, Jacob hoped he would stay. His KGB team would be a tremendous asset.

"As you all now know, President Mathias Goodman is the next target on these traitors' list. Their goal is only too obvious, to ignite a war between the United States and Russia to start a global nuclear war. These conspirators have only one instigating factor, money." Jacob leaned back in his chair, "We can only assume that the person who has contacted our very own Agency has contacted others like it, such as the KGB, and British MI6. This means that all of us have been pawns in a much bigger game."

Alexi picked up the conversation, his Russian accent following his words, "Jacob is correct. After our own internal investigation we could determine that there were several traitors in our midst. There goals were the same. I have only just now realized that by helping you can we help ourselves. These traitors threaten the fragile global peace that has remained intact for several decades. We do not wish your president dead by anyone's hands. He has strengthened his ties with Russia more than any who came before."

Madison interrupted, "If that were true, then why would the two nations go to war?"

Linda answered her question, "They would have no choice. The public outcry would be unbearable for one nation to ignore. Not only that, but if what we believe our own traitors are going to do, the NATO treaties will enact and declare war on Russia. Russia will obtain its allies in retaliation and global war would then be unavoidable."

Madison held her opinion back, hoping that people would not be so stupid as to go to war with nuclear superpowers, but as Linda had said, the treaties would be enforced.

As if Jacob was reading Madison's mind, "There would be no hope of our allies turning their backs on us or us to them. We are caught in these treaties."

"That's really dumb if you ask me." Madison said annoyed.

"It's what the world did after World War II, so that no one could again threaten the global peace." Alexi started, explaining why the treaties exist. "It was so that no one would threaten the west ever again. It also exists to protect the smaller nations who could not help themselves in the event of a Soviet invasion. Of course that nearly caused another war with the Soviet Union. Now the tensions are at that level once again. With these latest assassinations and catastrophes the world is readying for war once more. This war, between east and west, would be a war that no one can walk away from."

Linda asked the next question hanging in the air, "Why would anyone want to see that happen?"

Alexi turned to her and answered her in a polite, but cold tone, "Some people can become very rich and profit from war. The other horrifying version is that some people just want to see another war. If anyone survives, they will remember the name of whoever started the war. So perhaps this is done out of narcissism. Another outcome is that this is possibly the biggest terror event in mankind's history. Any way you put it, I don't like it."

Madison sat upright in her chair, "So how do we stop it?"

Jacob answered, "First, we need to stop Director Andrews and Harrison from carrying out their assassination attempt on President Goodman."

"That means we need to know when they will strike." Linda interjected. Jacob nodded at her words.

Kate spoke up, "From what I have been seeing in the news, the president is supposed to be making a speech on the White House lawn on the thirtieth. He is announcing a new proposal to seek further ties with Russia. Not only that, but we've made headlines for the third day in a row."

"That is going to make our jobs a lot more difficult then." Jacob said, "Alright, I'll take any ideas you guys have, because right now I'm empty. That and my last one didn't turn out how we all intended. I'm fairly certain that Andrews and Harrison will be attempting to execute their plan on that day. They would have to move up their timetable in order to keep us on our toes and to keep their secrets from spilling out lest we make their plot public. Which of course we can't do since there will be armed guards and bribed agents everywhere we go. So, I'm open to any suggestions."

The small group sat in silence for several minutes when Linda mumbled something. Jacob turned to her, "Have something Linda?"

"Maybe?" she said as she questioned herself.

Madison smiled for the first time in days, "You are the genius after all. You must have something."

Linda winked towards Madison's sarcastic compliment before she continued, "Well we all have to assume that those two know we are coming. They can't afford not to. That means they'll be expecting something out of us in an attempt to stop them. They would have to have teams placed at every entrance to the rally that they can. They all know what we look like now due to every television channel and media outlet."

Alexi asked, "So what is your suggestion?"

She turned to the group with a large smile, "It's so obvious guys. Who can get in with barely any restrictions?"

The other members exchanged confused glances between each other before turning back to Linda. Her smile became bigger, "Reporters! They gain access before anyone else in the crowd."

Alexi started to laugh, "That's so ridiculous it might just work! You, though, and I'm pointing to each of you, won't be able to enter. However, my men and I would be granted access because we have not yet been shown to every citizen in the States just yet!"

"So what do you expect us to do? Sit around while you guys take all the credit?" Madison asked with her temper rising.

Jacob put up a palm in front of her to cut down her attitude, "Kate, now is not the time to seek the glory. All that matters is that World War III is prevented. Besides, I have an idea that can get you and me in there discretely as well. We will meet up with Alexi and his men on the other side with the president in tow."

Madison cocked her head towards Fields, her temper almost forgotten while confusion took over, "What idea would that be?"

"You leave that to me." Jacob turned to his friend, "Alexi, I'm going to need a couple of your men."

Alexi complied with his friends request, "They are all in your debt, and as far as we're all concerned they're just as much your men as they are mine."

Madison turned her head towards Alexi as did Linda, both with the same question, "How do your own men owe their loyalty not only to you but to Jacob as well?"

The men gathered in the kitchen started laughing and one of them approached the table, Dimitri, "Well," he started with a rough Russian accent, "during joint operations, your man Fields led all of us through Hell and back. Alexi was always his second in command, even when Sampson was in the field. Those two have earned more of our respect than anyone could ever have."

Jacob felt a surge in pride at Dimitri's statement and replied humbly back, "You're a good soldier Dimitri, that's why I'm taking you with me on this next endeavor. That is if your commander is okay with it of course." Dimitri and Fields both glanced over to Alexi who sat with a smile and nodded.

"Wait, wait, wait!" Linda yelled, "How are you all going to portray reporters with those accents?"

Again the group of soldiers laughed and spoke to each other in their native tongue. Most of what they said made Fields laugh and wait for the expected as their conversation turned from Russian to rough English into excellent American English. There wasn't even a hint of their accents left.

Dimitri turned back to Linda and laughed, speaking without an accent, "Don't count us out just because we are Russian. I just like how our accent sounds when speaking English." He gave a wink to the speechless computer tech.

Jacob shook his head laughing, "Damn Russians, can't even trust them to speak their own damn language." The squad in the kitchen erupted with laughter at Fields' comment a few even clapped in agreement.

One of them shouted, "It's probably because of all the Vodka!" Again the group roared with laughter as the two American women shook their heads.

Madison, still shaking her head, "Stereotypical Russians."

Alexi glanced at her as she made her comment, "Best to get over it now, we're all you've got." He rose from his chair and strode over to his group of soldiers, "Dimitri is going with Fields on his errand, and I can think of no one else in this room that is qualified to help him! Stand to order! Another shout out like that and I will personally put my foot so far up your asses that your breath will smell like my boot! Stand to!"

As he was speaking the gang of soldiers nervously stood to immediate attention as their lack of discipline had gotten too far out of control. Alexi's voice became firmer, "This is not an agency like the CIA! We are Russian military! You will damn well act like it! We hold to discipline even in these relaxed situations! You have all been trained better! No more outbursts!"

The squad seemed to look down at their shame for being so unorderly. Alexi looked back to Madison, "Now that is what I like to call Russian discipline. Not stereotypical Russian bullshit!" He turned back to his men, "At ease boys, my point has been made." The group of men felt the thrill of relief as it was only a point to be made instead of actually being at the end of a tongue lashing.

Madison's jaw dropped, Alexi had given his men a verbal beating to prove a point of Russian discipline and to prove her ignorance wrong. In the time that she had known Alexi and his men over the last forty-eight hours she had been judgmental, but her opinion was changing. Alexi and his men had become huge assets and to her surprise, she started to like this gang of soldiers.

She held her head ashamed, "Your point has been well made Alexi. Forgive my ignorance."

Alexi patted her on the shoulder, "Most of your country thinks of us this way. It is only natural to fall into the peer pressure." He winked towards his men and they chuckled.

Jacob and Dimitri sat back amused as they watched everything transpire. They knew what was going to happen, but Jacob thought that his would be a good learning opportunity for both Kate and Linda.

"Let this be a lesson to both of you," Jacob started, "Never underestimate anyone. Enemy or friend, do not underestimate them. Period." He turned towards Alexi, "Now which one of these unruly bastards do you recommend coming with me and Dimitri?"

Alexi turned towards his men, "Ivan! Front and center!"

One of the shorter men came forward and stood at attention in front of the two commanders.

"Corporal Ivan reporting sir!" Ivan said as he saluted.

Alexi glanced towards Fields, "You already know what this Corporal is capable of Fields. I think you'll find him very useful."

Fields nodded his head, "I remember him." He looked towards Ivan, "Are you ready Corporal?"

Ivan's chest surged with pride, "Sir, yes sir!"

"Get your gear; you're heading out with me and Dimitri in five." Then Fields dismissed the man.

Madison rose from her chair as did Linda, "What do you have planned Fields? I think we should be in the loop on this one." Madison said with her determined voice.

"I agree Jacob. What do you have in mind?" Linda chimed.

"Just trust me okay? I'm going to bring back the key. You'll be pretty amazed with what I bring back if all goes according to plan." To Jacob's surprise it was Madison's face that lit up with concern and not Linda's, "Hey I'll be fine this time. These two have been through more combat than either of you, and I need Alexi here to lead you guys if we fail to return."

Kate let loose her unfiltered concern, “Then come back to us in once piece okay? I don’t want to lose you.”

Jacob’s eyes narrowed with confusion, but replied with his voice holding firm, “You won’t.”

Chapter Fifteen: Alexi Romanov

After Fields left with two of Alexi's men, the room became silent. Alexi broke the silence and gazed towards Madison, "What kind of look did I see just there comrade?" A smile broke on his lips.

Madison felt her cheeks blush, "What look!?"

Linda started to smile and took advantage of her friend's stunned state, "Yeah! What was that look Kate? Was that really concern I saw out of you? That whole 'come back to us' was really romantic." The Russian soldiers in the kitchen laughed at the short American's comment.

Kate's temper flared, "Okay, so I happen to have concern for a colleague. Let's not forget that he personally beat me up! Not only that, but he is responsible for losing my beautiful SUV, and he's the reason I got shot!"

Alexi responded, "Better to be shot than end up dead." He laughed as did his men.

"It was love at first punch!" cried a Russian soldier, and even Alexi could not contain his amusement as they burst out laughing some more.

"Oh screw all of you!" she yelled. She went over to the soldiers and grabbed the Vodka that they were passing around and took a swig of the liquid. The soldiers jaws dropped in surprise as did Linda's.

"Holy shit you drink?" Linda nearly screeched.

"I feel that the occasion calls for it."

Alexi leaned back in his chair, "Indeed it does my friend."

After finishing her taste of the alcohol she turned towards Alexi, "So what's your story Alexi? How did you end up here and helping all of us? Jacob told us how you two met, but wasn't very generous in sharing a lot of the details."

"That's a good question, Agent Madison, and one I will gladly share." He gestured for his men to gather around him and for Madison and Linda to return to their seats. He pointed to one of his men, "You, bring over a few glasses and a couple bottles of our country's favorite drink."

He poured each individual a glass and handed them out accordingly. His men were finally quiet with anticipation as their commander's voice began his tale.

Alexi started with a smile, "I started my association with Jacob before he was even in the CIA. As he probably told you, we held a big disdain towards one another. We hated the sight of each other simply because he was American, and I, a Russian."

He took a sip of his drink and cleared his throat, all eyes attentive on him, "Fields... heh. The man was a legend. Even in his service with the SEALS. He was the leader of SEAL team nine, one of the more covert and elite of the teams. Probably the best if you ask me. They went on the most dangerous missions, and each and every time they were successful. Though, I can only wonder as to how, because Fields always found himself in deeper and deeper shit. He always came out on top, no matter the odds. He and his team had a knack for survival."

He set down his glass and looked toward the interested faces, "Fields is probably the most dangerous man here. His skill is unmatched as I'm sure many of you know." He looked in Madison's direction.

Madison attempted to defend herself, "He got the jump on me! Okay? It's not like I was prepared for it!"

Alexi raised his hand, "Oh I'm quite sure agent Madison, but the point I'm trying to make is this. I am one of the most deadly men in Russia and the most skilled. So when I say that Jacob Fields is the most dangerous man in this room, I want you to fully understand my meaning."

Linda felt a chill go through her as Alexi spoke of Jacob. He wasn't wrong with his words. Linda had done background research on him dozens of times and had heard the stories.

"I can see right through you Ms. Baker. You know exactly what Fields is capable of." Alexi said as he observed Linda.

"Now, where was I?" He stared towards the ceiling to collect his bearings, "Oh yes. Jacob Fields, he was the talk around the forward operating base in Afghanistan. So naturally, I wanted to observe his skill set for myself and challenged him to a sparring match. It was supposed to be a fight with hands and feet, but turned into, well, pretty much a fight to the death had others not stopped us. Well, stopped him. He was severely beating me." He smiled as he recollected the event, "Jacob had speed over mine and his reflexes were unparalleled. I got in a few good hits, but the majority of them went to Fields."

Alexi stopped his story to take another sip of Vodka, after he put the drink down he continued, "After that little mishap we became something of mortal enemies at the base. Our soldiers got into fights constantly trying to prove who was better. To my surprise, we both encouraged it. We wanted to prove that either one of us could have the best men in the camp."

Something in Alexi changed, his voice became dark and filled with regret, "Then we heard the call, they had discovered the location of a terrorist we had codenamed Phoenix. They chose my team to go in and retrieve him. Finally we had the chance to prove ourselves better than your American top dog team. They put Fields' team on standby in case something went wrong. Of course, in my ignorance, I insisted that we wouldn't need them. The Blackhawks came down and took us to that small town of Bamyan. That town should be renamed Hell. Our twin Blackhawks were shot down as soon as we entered the area. Our enemy knew we were coming. One of the Blackhawks was completely obliterated while the other Blackhawk, mine and the men you see before you, held firm with its tail clipped. It was rapidly losing altitude and we were able to leap to the ground to safety before the pilot completely lost control and crashed, the poor American bastard. I felt terrible for his loss, he was a good man. After the crash we immediately came under fire from ISIS insurgents. There were dozens of them, possibly a little more than a hundred. I'm sure they thought that it was going to be Fields' team that was going to land there, but they weren't about to pass up on Russia's finest KGB team. We were able to fall back into a nearby building and used the helicopter for extra defenses. The machine gun on one of its sides was still operational and Dimitri and I went to retrieve it."

He paused to refill his drink, all the eyes around him were firmly fixed, and jaws were shut. His men looked at him with pride. Alexi smiled back at them, "Never enough vodka." His men chuckled at his joke as he continued, "Dimitri, poor Dimitri, was shot in the leg on our way back to the building. I had to haul him up and help him limp back towards our position. Our situation grew desperate, and reinforcements didn't seem to be coming. Our ammo for the machine gun was running low as well as that for our other firearms. The next thing we heard was rapid fire machine guns. Two Humvees approached our position and Jacob came in over the radio, 'Alexi Romanov! Your guardian angel has arrived!' Heh, I thought he was a prick, but I wasn't about to complain. Just as we were about to load up onto the trucks, one of them exploded, nearly killing the gunner, but he miraculously made it out of there okay. Jacob ordered the evacuation of the other Humvee before it too became the victim of the next RPG."

Alexi laughed, "Lucky for him everyone evacuated right before it blew up. He and his men joined us in our position and he thought we should have a forward post at the helicopter and drive some of the enemy back. Draw their fire away from the wounded. He volunteered to take up that position and put a few of his men to either side of the Humvees, making a crescent shape in front of our position. This allowed us to regain our composure and get more ammo from the vehicles. At the time it seemed our two squads could fight them off, but we realized we were both in over our heads. I tried calling for extraction, but they said it was going to take more time than we had."

Once again Alexi looked down in sadness, he gulped down the remainder of his drink, "Fields had only one bold option left. That's what his team's saying was, 'when options are low, go bold,' and that is exactly what he did. He called in wave after wave of air support and artillery. Within minutes F-22s were soaring overhead and dropping their payloads onto the insurgents. The artillery shells hit all around us, and it was very, very, successful. It made the insurgents think twice before they launched another assault on our position. During the strafing runs however, one pilot dropped his payload a little too close to our position." Alexi's voice trailed off as his eyes lit up and tears welled in the corners, "The payload killed two of Fields' men. Those two were men that Fields had been training with since his time in the Special Forces. They had been on every mission together. It was a very sad loss for him and I, my men could feel it too."

The men under Alexi's command were nodding their heads and some raised their glasses in salute to the fallen, "Fields was so shaken up after that that he was frozen in place. He couldn't find the motivation to continue. So I took charge. Finally, after another fifteen minutes of brutal ground combat the rescue squad finally came in and we were able to evacuate from that god forsaken place. It wasn't until we were on the helicopter that my men and I found out that Fields had disobeyed orders in order to come to our rescue. They stole a pair of Humvees and drove to our position without a second thought."

A smile came to Alexi and he sucked in a drought of air, "I comforted Jacob during that time, giving him a voice of encouragement and telling him that it wasn't his fault. After that incident we were brothers on the battlefield. Completely putting trust in one another. Of course, after that military disaster he went into the CIA and I went back to conducting KGB business. We conducted several co-op missions together. We have kept in touch ever since." He let out a long sigh and looked into Madison's eyes, "And that agent Madison, is my story."

Kate took a glance at the clock, it had been a few hours since Fields had left, "Thank you for telling us this Alexi. We know it couldn't have been easy."

"Well, we need to trust one another, Agent Madison." Alexi remarked.

"Yes we do," she said, agreeing, "But why wouldn't Jacob tell us his plan before he left?" Linda raised an eyebrow; it was the first time Kate had called their colleague Jacob.

Alexi chuckled, "It is very simple. Not everyone can know what he is thinking at first. I know I certainly didn't. It comes with working with him. You just have to learn to trust in his plans and pray by some miracle that they work." Alexi and his men started laughing again, "And they all do somehow!"

"So what you're telling me is that we have to just trust him?" Madison inquired.

Alexi smiled and nodded, "Yes. That is something that you need to learn. Trust. I know the last few weeks have not been easy on either of you and you may have some trust issues, but you can trust Fields."

The group jolted and pointed their weapons to the door as they heard it open. Fields, Dimitri, and Ivan walked in and immediately raised their hands.

"Are we interrupting something?" Fields asked, as everyone put their weapons down. Jacob put on a smile and revealed what he had planned to get.

Madison's eyes widened, "Oh, you have got to be kidding me."

Alexi and his men started laughing, "See agent Madison? It's all about trust." He rose and shook his head at Fields, "You are still one crazy son of a bitch, Jacob."

Chapter Sixteen: President Mathias Goodman

Oval Office

June 29

President Mathias Goodman sat at his appointed desk of the nation that had declared him fit to lead. His hair was combed over and he was wearing one of his favorite suites and ties. He sat patiently with two of his Secret Service body guards.

Soon the door to the office opened and Goodman's secretary, Stephanie, walked in through the opening, "Mr. President." She paused, waiting for Goodman to give a reaction. As he did she continued her message, "Director James Andrews is here to see you."

"Please send him in." Goodman said without much thought. Director Andrews had always been one to give much counsel during the tenuous peace with Russia. He had been one of the president's closest advisors on the issue.

After a few moments Andrews walked in with two other men. The president rose from his seat and offered his hand to Andrews. Andrews took it with a large smile on his face.

"Mr. President, allow me to introduce Lloyd Harrison and Joseph Ambrose." The president offered his hand towards the two

CIA members and they shook hands in the manner that depicted respect.

"A pleasure to meet you Harrison." He looked to Ambrose, "Ambrose, Please, both of you have a seat." He gestured to the chairs in front of him.

The trio sat gratefully, with Andrews taking the lead, "Mr. President. As you are aware, we have a fugitive running around by the name of Jacob Fields."

Goodman nodded his head acknowledging what Andrews was saying. "Yes you have kept me informed of the matter. Has he been finally dealt with?"

Ambrose took the stage next, "Actually sir that is why we are here. Mr. Fields has been very persistent and proven difficult to capture. To add insult to injury he has further corrupted three more agents of the CIA; Linda Baker, Keith Lincoln, and regretfully, Kathryn Madison."

"Regretfully?" Goodman asked with a scowl on his face.

Ambrose cleared his throat, "Yes, regretfully. She was on pace to being one of the best agents at the CIA. She was to take on a bigger role within a couple years." He scratched his eye before he spoke again, "Linda Baker was on track to taking over a management position."

"And Keith Lincoln?"

Harrison spoke, "Lincoln was apprehended in a firefight, but unfortunately he was killed. We couldn't get any information out of him before he died."

"It seems to me," Goodman said, "that this Fields has a commander's respect and loyalty."

Andrews was still sitting comfortably back in his chair, "He has indeed. However, the other reason we came here is to implore you not to give your speech tomorrow. The rally you hold will have thousands of people. I don't think we can protect you with that many civilians in the way Mr. President."

"That," Goodman raised a finger, "is not an option." He rose from his desk, put his hands behind his back, and looked through the window. "I will not let Jacob Fields bully me out of speaking tomorrow. The American people, yes, even the Russian people, must know that we are doing everything we can to prevent a war between our two nations." He turned back to the three men. "No, I will not cancel the rally. Make your preparations accordingly."

"Are you certain Mr. President?" Andrews inquired, putting on the best concerned look that he could.

"I am positive James." The president held out his hand for Andrews. Andrews rose and shook it firmly, "I appreciate all that you have done for me, but this needs to happen. You are all dismissed. Thank you."

The other two CIA members rose from their seats and shook the president's hand in turn. They waltzed out of the room and heard the door shut behind them.

Andrews turned to Ambrose, "Start making the preparations. If the president won't listen to us, then it is our job to protect him from his own stupidity." Ambrose quickly walked off leaving the other two alone outside of the Oval Office.

Harrison led Andrews out of the building and to their waiting car. Only once they were safely inside of the car did they dare speak to each other.

The agent turned to the Director, "What do you think Ambrose will set up for a defense?"

"I'm not sure, but he will inform us before it is carried out. I will ensure that your position is known to only a few. Remember, take the shot, and evacuate the premises. Fields is sure to be there and I pray we can find him before he puts a cork in our plan." Andrews smiled, "I can't wait to destroy everything that he has worked to achieve."

Harrison looked towards the fellow traitor, "Where do you think he will be?"

"That is the million dollar question Harrison. Even I am afraid of where he could be."

Sucking in a deep breath Harrison questioned his superior, "Are you still certain we should be doing this? I mean the president looks up to you as a mentor and highly regarded advisor, especially in regards to foreign relations. Are you sure you want to do this?"

"I am certain Harrison." Andrews said in a cold voice. The two men did not speak for the rest of the car ride to CIA headquarters.

Chapter Seventeen: Operation Siege

White House Lawn

June, 30

The crowd started to gather. The sun was high in the sky, raining down the hot light onto the strengthening crowd. People from all over the city and the nation had gathered to hear the president's plan for a continued world peace.

The speech wasn't set to commence for another hour, and tensions were running high in the crowd. Some in the crowd were already chanting. Others were simply onlookers waiting for the moment that their Commander in Chief would make his appearance on the podium.

One mile away, there was, glittering in the sunlight, a tall building right across from the Podium. Lloyd Harrison looked down the sight of his specially requisitioned Russian sniper rifle. It wasn't yet loaded, but Harrison could already feel the weight of burden on his shoulders. He had a clear line of sight to where the president would stand. The bullet proof glass would not present a problem for this high velocity gun, nor the slug it would release from the muzzle.

Harrison drew in his breath and let it out slowly, just waiting for his moment. The Director had accomplished his goal. Most of the agents and paid men would be scanning and combing the crowd for Fields, while a select few would guard Harrison's vantage point.

The Director had asked Ambrose to specifically make this a CIA only building. This would be the most logical target for an assassin, so of course the CIA would be responsible for "preventing" anything of the nature.

Harrison smiled to himself as the crowd gathered, *if only they knew what will happen in just an hour's time.*

He aimed down his scope again and pulled the trigger. There was a *click* that came from the hammer. Everything on the weapon was cleaned and prepared for the killing blow that must be delivered.

—∞—

Mathias Goodman sat in his office. He could feel the weight of a thousand burdens upon his shoulders. He wasn't about to let the world descend into chaos, but just being open like this could also be a sure way of starting it.

As Mathias sat alone with his thoughts, five members of the Secret Service walked in. The leader of the five agents spoke up, "Mr. President." Goodman turned to face him, "This is the detail that will be escorting you to the podium and will have their eyes on you like hawks."

Goodman smiled, "No one is taking any chances today, huh?"

The Secret Service man showed no sign of entertainment; he didn't smile at all, taking his job seriously above everything, "Not a single one, Mr. President. When you're ready, these four and I will be escorting you out to the stage. Once there, we will secure the podium area. After that we will receive the all clear signal from the surrounding areas. Only then will you reveal yourself."

Goodman smiled again, "Yes, yes. I know the procedure very well now, Gerald. Thank you."

Gerald bowed his head humbled, "I am simply doing my job sir, nothing more and nothing less." He turned to leave the room but turned back to face the president, "And sir?"

"Yes Gerald?"

"I admire you for what you are doing here today." With that, he left.

Mathias sighed and looked down at his long speech. It was to last forty-five minutes. Forty-five minutes of being an open target. He did not particularly like that, but it had to be done.

Fields is out there and he will do whatever he can to prevent this from being said, he will not get that chance.

Matias sighed once again. *This is going to be a very long day,* he thought.

—~—

"Harrison." The voice called out over his earpiece.

"Yes Director?"

"I have successfully deviated Mr. Ambrose from the rally. I have put him on a false lead of Fields. He led the only loyal team out of the crowd." There was a pause on the other side, "There is not a single reason why there should be one man to impede your progress or your shot."

"Yes sir." Harrison replied annoyed.

"In other words agent Harrison . . ."

"Sir?"

"No fuck ups."

A chill went down Harrison's spine, "Acknowledged," then the communication line went dead.

Harrison took in the warm air and steadied himself. His hands were shaking and his heart was pounding. He aimed down the sight and gazed at the waiting crowd that was still gathering. There were now over a few thousand down there.

He wiped his hands on his pants. They were sweating. He wiped more sweat off of his brow and put his eyes back through the scope. An idea hit him, locate Fields before anyone else. If nothing else it would pass the time.

His gun pointed from one person to the next as he surfed through the crowd with its scope. No luck. All the people's heads were turned away from him and there were too many. Wherever Fields was hiding he was doing it well.

Harrison put down the rifle and did a com check with the other team members on the floor. Making sure everyone reported in and there were no 'fuck ups.' He needed no make each agent and hired mercenary on his team know that he was in charge, and that orders would be followed to the letter. Everything needed to go according to plan or else it was their necks. *Nothing to do now, but wait.*

—ʌʌʌ—

"Mr. President?" Gerald said as he peaked into the room.

"Yes Gerald?"

"It's time."

"And so it is," the president said as he rose from his chair. He looked towards the Secret Service man and gave a shy nod, "Shall we present ourselves to the world?"

Gerald raised his arm and pointed to the door, indicating that the president should go first, "Indeed we shall. Remember what I told you. Do not make an appearance until we have heard the all clear."

Goodman patted his longtime friend on the shoulder, "As we have practiced hundreds of times. I will be fine. You just make sure my wife and daughter are secured inside of the White House with your best men."

"Already done, sir." Gerald said with pride.

"I can always count on you to be ready, can't I?"

"Always."

President Goodman walked out of the Oval Office and followed his escort to the opening to the White House lawn. He waited there as instructed with his escort.

Gerald motioned his men forward to take a look over the podium. As the secret service members walked out, there was a roar through the crowd. They all knew that the sight of them meant that their president and hero would be out at any moment.

Gerald put his hand to his earpiece, "Is he ready?"

Director Andrews came into Gerald's head, "Harrison is ready to take the shot. Remember; do not fire until I have given the order."

—w—

Director Andrews came onto Harrison's earpiece, "Harrison, Gerald is in position. He has given the all clear on the podium. He has even given us extra liberty by not actually putting bullet proof glass up, just the appearance of it. Report to all units and give the all clear signal back to him."

"Yes sir." He keyed his communications frequency and said into the earpiece, "All units return the all clear signal."

He stared through the scope at the podium where Gerald was standing. Gerald was looking straight at him it seemed, and he gave a nod to Harrison.

Harrison put down his gun just a little, *another traitor like me. What have I gotten myself into? No turning back now, no turning back.*

The crowd began to roar once more as the President of the United States, Matias Goodman, walked onto the stage. Harrison instinctively went for his sidearm at the unexpected cheering of the crowd. He was too nervous, too jumpy. He needed to calm down before he was able to take his shot.

He took in a deep breath to calm himself, and closed his eyes. He imagined that soon it would be all over. Soon he would be back at his job, a very rich man and he could get out of this whole system. His eyes burst open. That was his motivation, right there, get out.

Harrison picked up a handful of the rifle's bullets and he slid them into the loading chamber. The rifle was now fully loaded and he aimed down the sight, just waiting for the order that would change the entire world.

—∿∿—

Mathias looked at Gerald as we walked up to the waiting crowd, "Everything in order Gerald?"

"Perfectly." He lied.

Gerald looked back at the four mercenaries that he had hired. They each looked the part that he had assigned. In case the president somehow survived or got away, these four would go in and find his wife and daughter, and use them as leverage to bring him out of hiding. "Yes, everything is perfect."

Gerald gazed up at the building ahead of him. He could still see the glittering light bouncing off of Harrison's scope. He stared straight at it and nodded towards it. They were about to make history.

Mathias Goodman waved to the crowd and put on his best campaign smile. He had to hide the nervousness and insecurity that he was feeling. He buried it deep. That was one of the good things about being a politician; he could hide how he felt.

He approached the podium and looked through the glass towards the crowd; most of them were chanting his name. A lot of them were holding “No War” signs.

He looked to his left and right where his digital speech was located, then back to the crowd, “Good afternoon!” He shouted the statement and the response he got back was an overwhelming, “Good afternoon!”

Goodman couldn’t help, but smile at the returned statement, “Thank you all for coming here today. I have never seen so many people here when I’ve given a speech. Now, if I could just have this many people here for my next campaign rally that would be something!”

There was a ripple of laughter that went through the crowd. Not until everyone was dead silent did Goodman speak again. It was a good speech technique. It would gain everyone’s attention.

“You all know why I am here. Everyone expects me to announce a new plan. Well America, I have that new plan. I have a plan that will begin a brand new relationship with Russia and to make them one of our best allies in the entire world. I am announcing this new strengthening of ties because as everyone in the entire world knows, our nations have built up tensions. I won’t lie to the American people, these tensions are running high. In regards to those tensions, let me be the first and last person to tell you this, the United States of America did not participate in the bombing two years ago. The United States of America will never engage in any act of terrorism. We all have seen the horrors of terror."

"We still bear fresh scars of 9/11. Those scars still have yet to heal completely. That is why we, as Americans, will never engage in any act of terrorism. We know the horror first hand, more than any other nation. I, for one, will certainly not abide by it, nor will I be accused of it," He paused, "and neither should any of you! We are Americans. We do not encourage terrorism, we do not support terrorism, and we will not tolerate terrorism, foreign or domestic; we will stop them! Here today I will formally offer my hand to the Russian government and the Russian people to join me in this quest to end the horrors of terrorism."

—~—

Harrison looked on towards the president. He was giving a very passionate speech. Harrison almost believed that Mathias really could change how things were. Almost. But that future couldn't come to pass.

His earpiece broke in, "Harrison I am giving you the fire when ready order." Andrews own voice sounded nervous. Harrison's guess was that no one had found Fields or his crew yet.

Taking his rifle and aiming it steadily at the president, Harrison felt his nerves kick in once more. He found it difficult to aim the weapon. He closed his eyes and took in deep breaths in an attempt to calm himself. It almost worked. He looked back down the sight and had the president in his crosshairs.

"Remember Harrison, one shot and one kill. The panic that will follow will give you a clean getaway." Andrews' advice wasn't very helpful to Harrison. He already knew what would happen and what would follow after the shot.

Inquiring Harrison asked, "Have you any clue to the whereabouts of Fields yet?"

Demanding that Harrison step up his game, Andrews boomed into his mic, "Now Harrison. Now take the shot before he gets to the point of his speech." Harrison's finger slowly went to the trigger. He pulled it.

—ɯ—

Jacob Fields rushed in and tackled the president from behind. Everything seemed to be moving in slow motion. As Jacob tackled the president, a bullet flew over his head. He heard it wiz by and impact the building behind him. The glass in front of him shattered after the bullet's impact. Their guise as Secret Service members and mercenaries had paid off.

Madison drew her gun and aimed it at Gerald who was also reaching for his gun. She fired a trio of rounds in to him before he could do anything. He collapsed dead. The crowd had burst into a panic.

Alexi and Dimitri rushed in with their guns held at the ready. Everyone was in a crouch. Fields looked at the president, "Mr. President, I'm Jacob Fields and I've just saved your life." As he said that bullets burst overhead. More shots were being fired. *More than one shooter.*

Glancing at Alexi and Dimitri, "There are multiple teams on the ground! Need your men to form up and protect the podium!" Gunfire became abundantly clear as more and more bullets penetrated the sky and the building behind them. He looked at Kate, "You and I need to get him into the bunker!"

She nodded and inched her way toward the president. Taking him by the shoulder, "Mr. President are you okay?"

He was in shock, "You, you're the traitors."

"Not the time to discuss that Mr. President seeing as how we just saved your life!" More paid mercenaries emerged from the White House, but before they could fire upon the president Fields had taken his shots and the three men went down dead.

Still in shock Goodman mumbled, "My… my wife… daughter…"

"They're safe in the bunker!" Madison yelled over the hail of bullets. Alexi's men were in their positions and returning fire. "We need to get you in there now!"

Fields looked at Alexi and Dimitri still holding the stairways up to the podium, "We need to get him out of here! The White House is probably crawling with mercenaries and turncoats!"

Fields put his body over the president to protect him as Madison charged into the White House with her gun blazing. Alexi and Dimitri took up the rear.

They passed each room carefully, waiting for the expected ambush. As they rounded another corner three men jumped out from behind closed doors. Fields shoved the president to the ground before any of them could fire a shot towards him.

He lashed out with his palm and it collided with the closest man's jugular, permanently sealing the windpipe. He collapsed to his knees. The other two were dealt with by Madison and Alexi, both quickly put down. Fields picked the president back up and pressed on.

The team finally came to the elevator and waited for it to rise. There was no telling what would be on the other side. Alexi and Dimitri aimed down the hallway as Fields and Madison aimed at the oncoming elevator.

When it opened Linda Baker yelped in surprise, "Holy shit! Would you put those guns down!?"

The team complied and gathered into the elevator. Fields turned toward Linda, "So is everything secure down there?"

"Everyone and everything. The president's family is safe." Linda said.

Before the elevator went down Fields stepped off. They all looked at him with a questioning look. He looked at his comrades in arms, "I have to finish this before they get away."

As he said that Madison stepped off the elevator as well. "You're not doing it alone." She looked at the Russians "Alexi, Dimitri, it has been a pleasure."

The two nodded and Alexi replied, "I'll see you on the other side. We will keep your president and his family safe. You can count on that my friend." Then the elevator door closed.

"What's the plan Fields?"

"We kill them all."

—m—

Harrison was rushing down the stairs, thinking how dead he was going to be if he lived for the next few hours. His earpiece was a mess, dozens of their infiltrated men were screaming at the situation. Everyone was in disarray.

"Harrison! God damn it! I told you not to fuck it up and you did! Damn! Damn! Damn! Damn you Harrison!" Harrison didn't even notice all the curses that Andrews was screaming into his ear.

He thought of an idea, "Sir, we need to get out of here. We need to regroup! I have an idea on how we can turn this around!"

"An idea!? An *IDEA!? GO TO HELL HARRISON! I WILL SEND YOU THERE MYSELF!*" At that point Lloyd knew he was on his own. Never had he felt so scared, yet so free.

He tossed the earpiece out of the car window and he sped on. He knew his time was limited, but what was life if he had to live in fear? He had to enjoy everything while it lasted.

—m—

Linda made it back into the bunker with the president, Alexi and Dimitri. The bunker was a maze as they looked for the central room. Inside it there were large screens everywhere, but more importantly to the president, his family was safe and secure.

Running over to them, he nearly ran over his daughter. He held them very tightly with tears in his eyes asking them if they were okay. They were.

The president was holding his family tightly and muttering his private thanks to the group that had helped them all escape death. He looked up to Linda, "Who set all of this up?"

"I'm sorry Mr. President but you aren't going to like it."

"Tell me."

She hesitated before she responded. Andrews had been a mentor of the president, he knew a lot about foreign politics and how to maintain the peace. "Mr. President, its Director Andrews."

The president didn't scream out his revenge, nor did he yell out at Linda, he simply nodded in thanks and went back to hugging his family. Alexi was talking with his men and making sure the perimeter was clear. She looked back at the president and his family. They were all still hugging each other.

Linda Baker couldn't help but smile at the family before her. She opened up her laptop and turned to it. They had placed a tracker on Harrison's car and it was leaving the area rapidly. She had also given Fields' one so that she could track his position. She reached into her pocket, but she felt as though she was missing something. She felt around her pocket, but didn't find what she was looking for. Her car keys were missing.

"Oh that son of a bitch."

—∞—

The red Camaro zoomed out onto the street, rising above it for a brief moment before it collided back onto the pavement.

Madison looked over to Fields from the passenger seat, "You know Linda is going to kill you for stealing her car."

He pointed a finger towards Madison correcting her, "borrowed!" He put the car into third gear and sped faster after Harrison. "Madison I need you to ask Linda where Harrison is going! That tracker should still be on him!"

Madison complied, "Linda we need to find Harrison! Is that tracker of yours still working?"

Linda came back over their earpieces, "Of course it's still working! And when did you think it would be okay to take my car on this ridiculous chase!?"

Fields came in, "I'll explain that later! Right now I need you to tell me where Harrison is heading!" He quickly and expertly dodged his vehicle between cars and oncoming traffic.

"Give me a second!"

"We don't have a second! We need him now!"

"Take a left!"

Fields obeyed the directions given to him as he sped down another narrow street. Madison was holding on to the hand holder above the window.

Jacob saw this, "Kate I'm a great driver stop being nervous."

"I'm not nervous, I just hate it when I'm not the one who's driving! Look out!"

Eyes back on the road, Jacob slammed on the brakes and rolled to his right. He nearly rammed the car that had come to a complete stop. He shouted at the driver in his road rage, "Idiot! The light was green!"

"Yeah it's his fault for being a law abiding citizen." Madison said in a smart way. Fields just glared at her.

"Linda where is he?"

"He looks like he's attempting to leave the city! He's heading for the interstate! Turn Right!"

Fields turned right and put the Camaro into fourth gear, pushing it as fast as it could go. Linda's voice came back in his ear, "If you time it right he'll be passing by as you emerge from your road!"

A smiling Jacob looked toward Kate. She looked at him concerned, "What?"

In response Jacob put his foot on the gas, "We aren't letting him pass us."

Linda's voice on the other end became startled, "Jacob what the hell are you going to do?"

Fields looked at Kate, "This is gonna hurt." He pushed his foot further to the floor board; Madison prepared herself as Fields braced for the impact.

Harrison's car came into view and Fields smashed into it sending him barrel rolling across the road. The Camaro had its entire front smashed in. The air bags deployed, Jacob and Kate smacked their faces into them as glass shards went flying by. The duo obtained multiple cuts from the flying glass.

When the car stopped moving Fields and Madison laid back in their seats. Madison took in a few breaths and clutched at her stomach. Her bruises and wounds ached her, but not to the point where it was unbearable.

She looked at Fields, "I hate you."

He laughed a little, "I know."

To their surprise, Harrison emerged from his vehicle relatively intact. He was limping now, and running for the nearest building. It wasn't much, but it was the only shelter that he could afford, and have a few spare moments. Madison and Fields got out of the smoldering vehicle. They saw Harrison enter the building.

Madison turned her head towards Fields, "Do you think we should tell Linda?"

Clutching his left rib with his right hand Fields chuckled, "Oh hell no." He reached back into the Camaro and pulled out two Glocks. He tossed one to Madison, who pulled back the hammer, ready.

The two made haste as they entered the building. There were numerous civilians inside who noticed their guns, and were already holding up their hands. One of the elderly women in the room pointed to the door where they had seen someone else with a gun rush through. Fields gave his thanks and the two pounded through the door.

It led to a stairwell. There was blood on the rails, denoting where Harrison had been. The duo ran up the stairs following the trail. The blood led all the way to the roof.

Harrison was taking cover behind some of the pipes that provided the building with ventilation. He aimed his gun at the two agents rushing after him. He pulled his trigger and the bullets went zinging over their heads.

They ducked to avoid the projectiles and ran apart from each other to spread out. Madison returned her own volley to put Harrison's head down. Fields inched towards Harrison as he and Madison exchanged shots.

By the time Harrison noticed Fields he had run out of ammunition. Harrison pointed his gun at Fields, but only heard it click empty.

He put up his hands in defeat. He held his head in shame, waiting for the killing blow, but in never came. He looked back up at Fields, who was still holding his weapon and the hammer was back. All he needed to do was pull the trigger, but he didn't.

Fields, to Harrison's surprise, tossed the gun aside. Madison poked her head up, the two had squared off. Fields had his hands clenched as did Harrison. It seemed as though Harrison smiled, certain that his hand-to-hand combat could surpass that of Fields.

But Madison knew better. Kate lowered her gun and watched in the uneasy silence between the two men. Fields had more of a reason to kill Harrison than she did, but never had she seen Fields so angry. She was frightened herself, but Harrison's face was filled with overconfidence.

Harrison broke the silence, "You know I've been holding back right? I haven't shown you what I am truly capable of."

Fields voice became one of malice and hate, "I know that you are capable of taking innocent lives. I know that you are capable of deceiving everyone at the agency. I know that you are capable of dying." Madison grew chills on her arm.

Harrison's eyes squinted at Fields' last statement, "I will not die today!"

"Then you need to kill me, rookie." Jacob responded.

Without warning Harrison charged at Jacob with a blinding rage. He thought himself far above rookie status. He was the best! He would prove it against this man! He would prove it to the world that Lloyd Harrison had single handedly killed Jacob Fields!

The two men fell to the floor. Harrison delivered harsh blows to Fields' face. Jacob only took one punch and blocked the rest. Jacob put his right knee underneath the mass that was Lloyd and pushed out.

Harrison flew off of Fields and rolled as he hit the roof's floor. Jacob was back on his feet, fist ready to lash out as Harrison rose from his position. Fields noticed that the limp Harrison had, was on the right. He moved in quickly, ducked underneath Lloyd's blows, and struck the vulnerable point in his leg.

Lloyd yelped in pain and fell back. Harrison rolled before Fields could bring his foot on top of him and pin him. He successfully evaded Jacob's move, but it had been a farce. Jacob used his new momentum to fall on top of Harrison and elbow him in the sternum, but it didn't break. He didn't hit it with enough force to break the bone.

The air rushed out of Harrison. He was gasping for breath, but his strength had not left him yet. Lloyd used much of his strength to hit Fields in the ear.

The blow caused Fields to roll off of Harrison in a fit of unexpected pain. The two men were on their hands and knees, panting heavily.

Fields looked over to him, "You can still put up a fight," He held his breath as he struggled to rise, "but I will end this here and now."

Lloyd was also struggling to get up, but he was slower than Fields, "I won't . . . I can't . . ."

Harrison collapsed onto the ground defeated and he turned over. Fields limped to Harrison and stood over him.

Harrison looked his enemy in the eyes, "You have to kill me. He . . . He'll come for us . . . and now he'll come for you."

"Who will?" Fields asked.

He spit out blood before he responded, "You don't know do you? You couldn't. I mean, how could you?"

Madison had walked next to Fields and pointed her gun straight down towards the dying man. Jacob realized that he had indeed broken Harrison's sternum. Madison saw it too and lowered her weapon. It was killing him, but slowly.

Jacob violently grabbed Harrison's collar, "What are you talking about!? We already know that Andrews is behind it all!"

Harrison laughed through his bloody teeth, "Andrews? He's . . . just . . . another . . . pawn in . . . the game."

"What game?" Jacob demanded.

But the question came too late. Harrison convulsed and his eyes glazed over. Death overcame him as the convulsions stopped, and Jacob let go of the hold he had on Harrison's collar. Jacob put his hand on the traitor's face and closed Lloyd's eyes. Fields stepped away, but Madison kept staring at the dead body before her.

Without looking at Fields she called to him, "And just like that . . . it's over?" A fire was burning inside her. She couldn't face that the man who had betrayed her was finally dead, but not by her own hands. She had wanted to take part. A thought came to her; no she was glad she hadn't taken revenge. Revenge was a path to ruin. This was justice that she and Fields had done.

Fields glanced over his shoulder, "Agent Madison. This isn't over yet. We still have to deal with James Andrews, and I think I may know where to find him."

—~~—

Madison and Fields approached the White House where there were hundreds of armed personnel. They all raised their weapons on their approach. One of the lieutenants stepped forward.

He spoke loudly, "Jacob Fields and Kathryn Madison, you are hereby under arrest for treason against the United States of

America, murder, assault, and involvement in a conspiracy involving the killing of the president of the United States."

The duo raised their hands. They had no other option but to comply. As the lieutenant approached so did a very tall man with short hair and a hooked nose.

His veins seemed to pop out of his neck, "There will be no such charges! These two are damn heroes!" The soldier backed down before he did anything stupid. The man in front was obviously a higher rank and possessed with authority. Joseph Ambrose approached the two, "The president has given me direct orders to see you both to him. Follow me."

Jacob and Kate looked at each other confused, but obeyed his orders. The Oval Office soon appeared in front of them. There were rows of people on either side of the two agents, all of them clapping as they approached.

The door opened and they walked in. The people present surprised them both. The president was there, obviously, but so was his family. Linda was there, so was Alexi and all of his Russian men.

Linda approached the pair, her face red with anger, but she also couldn't help but be glad at the sight of them, "You two owe me a brand new car! You had no right! But damn am I happy to see you two!"

Fields and Madison smiled, they couldn't help it. After the day that they had been through, the last thing they expected was for a short green-eyed genius yell at and congratulate them at the same time.

Alexi rose next, as did his men. He held out his hand in congratulation, "You are one crazy bastard Fields, but I've never met anyone else who could have accomplished what you and Kate did today."

Jacob took it, "Alexi, I can only thank you and your men for everything you have done." Alexi and his men nodded humbly.

The next person who went to greet the duo was President Mathias Goodman. He offered his hand and Madison took it first, then Jacob. His face had a broad smile on it. It seemed that he was struggling to find words for the two. Then he just laughed a little.

He turned to his wife and daughter, then back to Jacob and Kate, "These two and I cannot thank you enough for the service that you have performed today. You are heroes today. As a thank you for your deeds, I am granting all of you a full presidential pardon."

Relief seemed to wash over Kate. She had been forgiven in that moment for what she had done in the service of her country. Her heart was filled with pride. As she glanced at Jacob, she noticed that he still had a stone hard face on.

The president noticed this as well. Mathias walked straight in front of Jacob, "Does this not please you agent Fields? You have been pardoned."

His stone eyes looked back at the president, "Sir, I am not displeased by what you have done for me and my group of loyalists. I need to ask you something in return."

"Anything agent Fields."

"James Andrews is still out there. Give me the order. I need to finish this, with Madison." Kate was shocked. Jacob had never asked anyone to join him on a mission. Everyone volunteered to offer their help to Fields, not the other way around.

"Why just her and not the rest of them, agent Fields?" Mathias asked.

Jacob's stare did not falter, "Because she knows firsthand what it feels like, as I do, to be betrayed. There is nothing better than a little payback."

Mathias was nodding at him. He fully understood what Jacob was asking. He was going to kill James Andrews, not bring him in to answer for his crimes. He understood their need for revenge, but as a president he could never allow such a thing.

The president turned towards his bodyguards, "It seems that we have yet to locate Jacob Fields and Kathryn Madison. I hope they do return here tomorrow. I have much to ask of them." He turned towards the two agents who fully understood his meaning. They shook his hand in thanks and left. They had a day at most to find the traitor, Andrews.

As they were leaving, Madison asked Jacob, "So you actually want me along for this one?"

"I've wanted you to be next to me the entire time we've been together. You're a good agent Madison, and I'm going to teach you everything I know."

A surge of pride went through Madison. Jacob had just given her one of the best compliments she had heard. She was good enough to be next to the most dangerous and skilled person in the world. Then it hit her that he was going to teach her a few things when all this was over. A smile grew on her face, but that wasn't all, something deep inside her bubbled to the surface. She blushed. She not only looked up to Fields but she actually liked him.

"Are you ready Kate?"

"I'm ready Jake."

Jacob noticed what she called him, but he liked it. The two had finally developed a bond, and it only appeared to be growing. Fields had always known such attachments to be a weakness, but this seemed different. He shook his head to clear it, now wasn't the time for such thoughts.

"Let's go kill a traitor."

Chapter Eighteen: Retribution

Harrison's House

Night June 30

Director Andrews and a team of mercenaries infiltrated his fellow conspirator's house. He heard earlier that evening that Lloyd Harrison had been killed and that Jacob Fields would be on his trail soon enough. James started to panic. He needed to erase everything that could trace back to his employer. Andrews knew he was already a dead man walking, but maybe if he helped cover HIS, tracks there could be a chance!

The team combed every inch of the house deleting all of the evidence. They removed every trace that Harrison or that Andrews had been here. Andrews' heart was still pounding. His hands were sweating and shaking. He did a walky-talky check every five minutes to be sure that everyone was still with him and that no suspicious activity had been seen.

He called out another com check, but only five out of the six reported in. Andrews realized he didn't hear from Evans. He called out again, but only five responses came back.

The walky-talky buzzed and a familiar voice came through, "Hello Director." It wasn't Evans.

Andrews' heart sank in his chest, "Fields?"

"So glad you remember me, Director. I feel honored that a man of your unique stature would remember me."

Anger gripped the Director, but he held it back, "You were the finest asset I ever had trained Jacob. You were my best man, my top assassin. I wonder how your friends would respond if they figured out how many men and women you killed for me."

The walky-talky was silent for a time, but Jacob's voice came booming, "That was another time, another life. I died remember?"

"And you're still the assassin Jacob. You're still a tool. You'll always be an assassin. You were my greatest student. So now will you demonstrate all you've been taught? Will you strike down your teacher?"

The walky-talky buzzed one last time, "You know I won't hesitate to kill you. And you're right. I will always be an assassin. You taught me that. I hope you've made your peace with God." Then the walky-talky went silent.

Andrews turned to his few remaining loyal agents, "Everyone get ready! Fields is out there! Don't you idiots get it!? All of your lives are at stake!" They looked at him confused, they didn't understand the danger that they were all in. Jacob Fields couldn't be that dangerous could he?

A shudder went through Andrews. He had never been so scared in his life. He was always the intimidator not the other way around. He didn't know how to react. He looked towards the mercenaries still following his lead, but James could see the startled looks on their faces. All they could do now was wait for the end.

—ʬ—

Jacob Fields was hefting a SCAR that Joseph Ambrose had specifically requisitioned for Jacob. The weight was so familiar to him after all his years in the marines and the SEALS. The scope on it was perfectly adjusted the way Fields liked it. He had given another SCAR to Madison. She wasn't yet fully comfortable with the weapon, but she'd get used to it after her training under Fields was complete.

Jacob finished his conversation with Andrews and threw the walky-talky far away.

"What was that all about Jake?" she asked very concerned.

He gazed at her in a new light. Madison had started calling him Jake. No one had done that before, and from what he heard from Madison, it was huge. She never used first names, let alone nicknames. He was angry with Andrews for bringing up his past, "Let's finish this and then I'll tell you everything you want to know. Keep your head in the game. No distractions. Distractions get you killed, first lesson."

Madison realized that Jacob was using this as a training lesson for her. She could respect that. She cleared her head by closing her eyes and taking a deep breath. She opened them and saw that Fields was checking his weapon. She did the same. *Care for a piece of equipment like it was a child,* he had told her before they came here.

"Are you ready Kate?" Jacob implored.

"As ready as I'll ever be."

Jacob nodded his head and moved forward in a crouch. He was moving at a slower than normal pace to muffle the sound of his footsteps. Madison was doing the same, copying his every move. *Good, the girl caught on quick.*

Another man popped into their view, he was armed to the teeth, but he failed to notice the pair of agents. Jacob silently slung his rifle behind his back and drew his long knife. It was a Ka-Bar, standard issue military.

Jacob crept up on the unsuspecting man. He rose and with lightning quick hands, catching the man's mouth with his left hand and taking the knife in his right hand and sliding it across the mercenary's throat. The blood oozed from the wound, but he was unable to call out for help. He went to his knees still holding his own throat and convulsed until he died.

Jacob wiped his blade on his victim's shirt. He looked over to Madison and held up four fingers, meaning four more men inside. Kate acknowledged it with a nod.

The two approached a window, the very same one that Jacob had broken into only a few days before. He took his SCAR off his shoulder and aimed it through the window. Madison flanked the mercenaries inside by taking up another window adjacent to the one Fields was at. Jacob was supposed to fire the first shot.

He waited until all four men entered his vision. Jacob had also given a strict instruction that Andrews was not to be touched.

The crosshairs lined up with what seemed to be the mercenary leader. Jacob squeezed the trigger and the SCAR's automatic burst illuminated the room. The leader went down under the hail of gunfire. He heard Madison's weapon discharge not long after Jacob's had. Three more went down. The only person left alive was the Director.

Madison and Fields hopped into the room. They found a terrified and nervous James Andrews. He had been shaking the entire time. He knew that this was the end.

Andrews raised his hands, "Well Fields, we both knew it would end like this."

"No Director, I don't think so." Jacob replied. He looked at the aging man. He was terrified to lose his life. He pointed to the floor and the Director went to his knees and Madison zip-tied his hands behind his back. "If you're so scared to lose your life, you wouldn't have participated in the actions that you have."

The Director became furious, "You have no idea how terrified I am! Not only because you're here, but even if you let me live

He'll kill me anyway!" He was shouting at the top of his lungs. Jacob punched him to silence him, that or out of anger, all he knew was that it was gratifying.

"Keep your damn voice down." Jacob said menacingly.

Andrews looked back to Jacob, "How did you find me? Did I really teach you that well?"

"It's simple really, and yes you've taught me a thing or two." He paused finding the right words, "I assumed that you would find out that Harrison had been killed. After all, you two had a lovers' quarrel after you failed to kill the president. Everyone wearing an earpiece heard that. As he lay dying he spoke of a third person, someone who was in charge, even in charge of you. You just confirmed that you were already a dead man, but not by me. I knew that Harrison would have evidence to link everything back to your employer. So enlighten me. Who's in charge?"

Andrews shuddered again. *My God he really is nervous!*

James looked at the ground and he started a pathetic laugh, "You know Jacob, it's kind of ironic. The hunter becomes the hunted!"

"How?"

"Because since you've ruined all his planning, the planning of the last five to ten years, He'll come after you."

"I'll kill him first."

Andrews laughed again, "Ha! You can't kill him! He's everywhere! His agents! His spies!"

"Who is he!?" Jacob yelled into Andrews' face. Madison stepped back a little from Jacob. Fields angry wasn't a man to be near.

"You already know of him! Hell everyone does!"

“Why does he intimidate you so much? Who is he?” Jacob demanded.

Andrews’ eyes bulged with fear, “He intimidates me because that’s how he gets people to turn to his side! Intimidation! Life or death! He gives you the option, you either join him and live to earn a great paycheck or you die! Plain and simple! His agents, his army of intelligence and Special Forces! How could you not be afraid of this man!?”

Jacob closed in on Andrews face until there was merely an inch apart from each other, “Tell me his name! I can make your death painful or quick! You choose!”

“I just have his alias! That’s all I have I swear!” Andrews screamed back.

“What is it!?” Jacob demanded again.

“You have angered him greatly Jacob! He will see you dead for all of your meddling in his plans! He will burn you!” Jacob looked down at the Director and saw that he had wet himself. Was the man so terrified of his employer?

Jacob had only one option left, violence. He punched Andrews in the gut as hard as he could without damaging any of the internal organs, “Tell me what I need to know!” He punched him again. Madison turned away, intimidation had never been one of her strong suits and she couldn’t watch it.

“I need you to tell me his name! Tell me everything you know about him!” Andrews seemed to give in.

When she turned back around she saw Andrews leaning in to whisper into Jacob’s ear. She didn’t hear what was said, but the look on Jacob’s face was a clear sign that it wasn’t good.

He drew out his Ka-Bar from its sheathe and cut off the zip-ties holding the Director.

Kate raised her hands and was about to yell at Fields, but Jacob put up a finger to silence her. The Director pulled out his hands in fear.

"No! No! NO! You have to kill me Jacob! You have no idea what he'll do to me if he catches me!"

Jacob looked over his shoulder, "That is not my concern Director. It's yours. Go home." Kate was in shock, but followed Jacob's lead. She ran to catch up with him. Behind her, she only heard the loud cursing of the Director.

The two hopped into Kate's black SUV. Jacob was driving and Kate was in the passenger seat. The pair remained quiet for a time before Jacob finally said something, "So do you have any questions you want to ask me?"

"Only about a hundred." Kate said.

Jacob smiled his boyish grin, "I figured you would. Go ahead."

Kate couldn't resist her first instinct of curiosity, "First off, what did Andrews tell you?"

It seemed as though Jacob went pale. His fear was becoming very apparent.

"He only gave me an alias, but we both know it."

"Jake, what was it?" Madison pushed.

Jacob looked over to her. It made her all the more unsettled when she saw the fear in his eyes. "He muttered only a single name. Phoenix."

Kate's jaw dropped in surprise, "Phoenix? As in the man from Bamyan, Phoenix?"

Fields only nodded in response. His hands were firmly gripped to the steering wheel. His knuckles were white with the tension. Jacob's broad shoulders were reeling back as if he were about to punch something. His temper had nearly burst, but he held it all back.

"The very same. Had I known then what I do now . . ." his voice trailed off. His memories from that hell hole had taken a hold of him. His eyes seemed to become distant. Suddenly he was back in the present. He shook his head trying to clear it.

Madison broke the uneasy silence, "Why did you let Andrews go?"

Jacob took his time, "I didn't. Not really. Those men will come for him and probably torture him to gain as much info on me and you as they can, but I left a surprise for him."

"A surprise?"

"You'll see," he said.

She nodded, "And what about the things that you have done?

He looked down in regret it seemed, "Kate I have done a lot of terrible things. I am partly to blame that Andrews came this far. I killed for him before, but that was when I thought I was doing just my duty. It seemed that I was doing the right thing. I killed important political figures, but only because I was told to. I'm a soldier and I obeyed orders. I was a fool, but I wised up eventually. I figured out that these targets weren't just because they had done bad things; they were causing global problems. By the time I asked, it had been too late. I can only guess as to why the Phoenix had waited two years after my disappearance to strike at our president. It doesn't make sense, but I'll find that out eventually."

"So," She started, "you really are an assassin? The world's greatest?"

"So the stories say," he paused, "but that doesn't make me any less human. I have hopes and dreams. I'm not always an assassin, but I'm not always a kind and gentle heart. I need to be who I need to be, easy as that." He looked at Kate with concerned eyes, "I'll never let anything happen to you Kate. I promise."

Something inside Fields told him to protect Kate with his life. Was it his duty or his rising feelings? He didn't know, nor did he care. All he cared about in that moment was Kathryn Madison, the extraordinary woman who had saved his soul.

—∞—

The fear was not wearing off of Andrews. He sat in the empty house for a couple more hours contemplating his options. He realized he had none as he was sitting there. He decided to take Fields advice and go home.

Upon entering the building he called home, he knew something was amiss. He couldn't place his finger on it, but inside something wasn't right. He advanced slowly forward, his nerves taking control of his body as he shivered uncontrollably.

His mind couldn't help but think that the Phoenix's agents had already been here and were waiting for him. He didn't know how much time he had. James ran into his study and locked the door.

He looked around, being careful not to walk into any traps. The last thing he wanted was to be strangled from behind. That was one of the chief ways that the Phoenix killed insubordinates or failures.

Andrews approached the desk. On top of it was a note. His curiosity got the better of him as he reached a shaky hand towards it. He picked it up and opened the note it simply read:

Fuck you

-JF

James looked down and saw a timer only set for a couple of seconds. It was attached to a bomb. He chuckled at the irony, and the entire building exploded into a ball of flame.

—ꟷ—

Jacob and Kate had parked in front of Andrews' house. They waited a few hours until finally the Director himself showed up at his residence.

Madison voiced a question, "Do you think he has any idea what is going to happen to him?"

"Not a chance in Hell," Jacob said.

They sat in a comfortable silence. Both people felt that they didn't need to talk. They had an understanding and that was the comfort between the two. It was pleasant.

Jacob inhaled as he looked down on his own hand held timer. Andrews had read the note and triggered the bomb to blow. *Two... one...* and the entire block was alight with the flames that burst into view from Andrews' house.

"There, I kept my end of the bargain Andrews. Thanks for teaching me."

"You still thank him for turning you into a weapon?" Madison asked.

"It's the reason I'm still alive as are the rest of you. So yes I will thank him for that one last thing," Jacob said. "He also hired you." He smiled with the last statement, and Kate smiled too.

She spoke up, "Let's get out of here."

"Agreed."

—ꟷ—

Somewhere in Afghanistan

The man had been in a rage all day, after he had learned the news that all his years of careful planning had been undone by a small group of patriots. The table where he was sitting was supposed to be a table of victory. The meal he was eating should have been sweet not sour. This was what defeat felt like he mused. He never liked losing.

The news came in to him as he was sleeping. He nearly had the messenger strangled for being the bearer of this awful outcome. The insolence! The outrageous things that had come! How vulnerable he felt! PAH! *I am untouchable.*

He was fairly confident that everyone who knew how to contact him or link anything to him was severely destroyed. Andrews had cost him much. He was his most prized tool. He could accomplish anything. The man had a talent for manipulation and intimidation. But he was gone. A well placed spy had seen his home explode.

The Phoenix had undoubtedly underestimated the man they called Jacob Fields. He had proven to be a major thorn in his organization's side, and it was only going deeper. Like a bullet that continued to travel through to the heart. He needed a way to prevent this man from his further meddling, but that would come in its own time. *Patience.*

If anything in this line of work had taught him something it was patience. Plans would come to their fruition in their own time. He needed time to recognize Fields for what he was and what he was capable of. Only then can the Phoenix strike.

The Phoenix smiled, and when the time was right he would destroy everything that Fields had built. In return for the great sins he has caused against the Phoenix. The food turned sweeter with the thought. Yes, victory will come on its own terms.

Chapter Nineteen: Home

CIA Headquarters

July 1

Jacob Fields stood outside the building. He looked up at it with all its brilliance. Everyone who was gathering inside thought that it was over. No, it was far from over. Only Jacob and Kate knew that. Jacob didn't even want her involved. The adventure may cost her, her life. Fields was willing to sacrifice that, but was Madison? As for the others, would they want to join him as well? *In time, forget it now. Be here in the present,* he thought.

He stepped gently forward and pushed himself through the doors that opened before him. There was not a single employee missing as they gathered around Jacob. They were all clapping and congratulating him, patting him on the shoulder and wanting to shake his hand. He tolerated it, but he knew he was no hero. He was just an assassin. A tool. *No, you're not. Kate has taught you that.* He smiled, he was a human being. That's who he was.

Joseph Ambrose was at the end of the crowd. He also shook Jacob's hand and gave him a thank you. Jacob also noticed that Ambrose had been promoted to the Director of the CIA. *Good, a man that knows what he's doing.* Jacob also gave his congratulations on his promotion.

Ambrose asked him a question that he barely heart, "Would you step in to my office?" Jacob nodded.

Once safely in the sound proof room Ambrose motioned for Jacob to take a seat. He took it.

Ambrose let out a long sigh, "Who would have thought that this is where we would end up? I'm congratulating you when just yesterday I was ordered to kill you. Heh, the situation was extremely . . . fluid." He smiled. Ambrose never smiled; at least that's what Kate said about the man.

"It is a strange world that we live it, sir," Jacob said.

Ambrose grinned again, "It is indeed." He looked down towards his desk and then back at Fields, "The president has also asked for you to be his personal Secret Service bodyguard."

Jacob raised an eyebrow, "Did he?"

"It seems that you have had quite the impression on President Goodman. You would be taking over Gerald's job." Fields' eyebrows creased not understanding. "The one that agent Madison killed on the stage." Jacob gave a silent, "Oh."

"With all due respect, I do not like babysitting sir," Jacob said defiantly.

Ambrose looked Jacob straight in the eyes, "I was hoping you'd say that. We've lost too many men and women during this conspiracy, and I'm not about to lose the best man I have." He laughed, "And I thought I was going to have to give you some long and drawn out speech to convince you to stay."

"No sir."

"Good." He pulled out a file from his drawer. "Now, before coming in here you had mentioned something about a man called, 'the Phoenix' is that correct?"

Jacob nodded his head in confirmation.

"Good." He planted the file in front of Jacob, it was titled, *The Phoenix*. "This is everything we have on the man. Keep in mind that it's not much, but if you want to go after this man, know that the CIA will be behind you as well. This is a matter of national security, so I won't let you go alone. You will report directly to me. I will let you choose your team. We need to gather intelligence and everything that we can before we pursue this man to whatever hellhole that he is hiding in. Understood?"

"Perfectly sir."

"You're dismissed."

Jacob rose and turned on his heel. He had a smile on his face; finally a chance to go after the real problem. He saw Kate from the corner of his eye and he winked at her. The last time he did that she put a bullet into his shoulder. He laughed to himself. *How things change.*

He went over to his desk. They had given him his old one and had his name back on it. *Ah, home.* He thought.

—ᨓ—

Madison watched Fields from her desk. He seemed happy to be back. The familiarity of his surroundings, the people . . . it must have been an overwhelming feeling for him. He was getting handshakes from a lot of the people and Kate couldn't help but smile. He was the single reason that two of the world's greatest nations hadn't gone to war. *Give yourself some credit! He needed you!* She smiled at her self-confidence. It was finally and gradually returning.

She noticed Jacob get up from his seat and stride over to where she was sitting. He was grinning that damned stupid boyish grin he always had, but Kate liked it.

"I guess congratulations are in order, huh Fields?" She smiled at him.

He nodded his head, "It would seem that way, but I actually came here to thank you. I couldn't have done it without you, or Linda, and Alexi. I owe you guys a lot. So if you ever need anything just ask."

"Well you did promise me one thing."

"I did?" He frowned struggling to remember, but his smile came back instantly, "Yes I did, didn't I?"

"So, what do I need to learn?"

"A lot." He laughed.

She put her head down smiling before she looked back up into Fields eyes, "When do we start?"

"Soon," He said plainly. He put a large case file on Kate's desk it said, *Phoenix*. She looked back up at Fields who continued, "But first, we have a lot of work to do."

"I thought we were done with all the work?"

Fields laughed a long laugh, "Oh Agent Madison," he smiled that boyish grin, "We're just getting started."

CPSIA information can be obtained at www.ICGtesting.com
Printed in the USA
BVOW06s1236170216

437019BV00009B/127/P